Suddenly a blinding flash of light caused them to gasp.

For a confused moment Ryan thought that someone had taken a picture of them before he realized it was lightning. In the next instant, Billy was on his feet.

"Did you see that animal?" Chris jumped up, looking wildly around him.

Before Billy could reply, a bone-chilling howl rang out, causing Ryan to scream in sheer terror. Turning their heads toward the sound, the boys saw the distant figure of a wolflike creature baring its fangs, illuminated by the next flash of lightning. The shock was so great that Ryan felt as if the breath had been knocked out of him. "A werewolf!" Chris whispered.

Ryan shook his head. "No, it's impossible."

The TWIN Connection

MYSTERY AT MAGUIRE'S FARM
Adam Mills

BALLANTINE BOOKS ● NEW YORK

To the gang in Kansas City

Twin Connection

RLI: $\dfrac{\text{VL: 5 \& up}}{\text{IL: 5 \& up}}$

Copyright © 1988 by The Jeffrey Weiss Group, Inc. & Helen Pyne

Produced by The Jeffrey Weiss Group, Inc.
133 Fifth Avenue
New York, New York 10003

Library of Congress Catalog Card Number: 88-91549

ISBN: 0-345-35128-2

Manufactured in the United States of America

First Edition: November 1988

ONE

Pedaling furiously, Ryan Taylor felt a surge of energy as he looked up and saw the crest of the hill approaching. He was almost there!

But before he even had a chance to turn and look, he sensed someone behind him. A moment later he saw Chris's red bike out of the corner of his eye and heard his brother's laughter as he cried out, "You're running out of steam, pal. I'm catching up!"

Ryan didn't waste his energy on a reply. Gritting his teeth against the pain in his lungs, he pumped with all his might, pushing down faster and faster against the pedals. Up and up and up he rode—and finally over!

With a whoop of joy, Ryan glanced back at his brother who was still a full five yards behind him. The look on his brother's face told Ryan something he already knew—Chris wasn't used to defeat.

"Don't get a swelled head. You just got lucky, Shortie," Chris huffed. *I don't mind being three inches shorter than Chris*, Ryan thought to himself, grinning happily, *as long as I can beat him in a bicycle race.*

"What's the matter, you big lug?" he retorted. "Did those size ten feet of yours get caught in the spokes?"

"I gave you a break, shrimp! And it's not going to happen again!"

Ryan laughed, knowing full well that losing on purpose was one thing his competitive brother would *never* do. "You expect me to believe that," he cried, gleefully, as Chris shook his fist in the air.

Coasting down the hill, Ryan opened his mouth to let the wind rush in, enjoying its coolness against his face and across his bare arms. This part of the ride felt like flying. The wide open space stretching out on either side of him made Ryan feel free as a bird—he loved the Kansas countryside, the rows of wheat and corn, the green fields and apple orchards. In the distance he could see Lake Watanabe, shimmering under the light of the midday sun.

Chris pulled up beside Ryan, and they walked their bikes down the dirt road until they reached the farm where their friend, Billy Maguire, lived.

"Maybe I'll let you get even with me tomorrow in mud Frisbee," Ryan said cheerfully.

"Awww, what a pal. I bet you'll let me win, too," Chris replied, grinning.

"I know I can beat you if I really want to," Ryan said seriously. He held up an arm and flexed his muscles. "And I know I'm growing. I bet by Christmas I'll be as tall as you and you'll be sorry you ever so much as mentioned my height."

"Dream on, big brother," Chris laughed. "You

may be three minutes older but you'll never be as tall as me—not with the way I've been putting away the chow."

Ryan rolled his eyes, remembering the three full plates of spaghetti his brother had eaten the night before. "Then I'll just have to mix Mom's Miracle Grow into your food and speed up the process. I'll turn you into a freak of nature," he threatened.

Chris laughed again and pulled off the Royals baseball cap he wore to wipe his freckled face. Blonder and more fair-skinned than his brother, he always felt the sun first.

"Being tall does have its benefits. It's just that you're not taking advantage of them," Ryan began mischievously.

"What do you mean?" Chris asked, his eyes narrowing.

"Well, you really blew it this summer when that cute high school lifeguard was interested in you."

Chris blushed. "What was I supposed to do? Tell her that I'm thirteen, not sixteen like she thought? How was I going to pick her up for that party she asked me to? Have Dad chauffeur us both ways? That would have impressed her. Or should I have just taken the car? After all, Billy taught us to drive last summer," Chris said sarcastically.

Ryan chuckled. "Don't get so huffy. You're right—it was doomed from the start."

Chris groaned. "Let's drop the subject. I'd like to have fun today, and that means not talking about girls."

"Okay, I'll drop it," Ryan said. "But you don't

need to worry. Girls are only attracted to you until you open your mouth."

"Just because you read all the time doesn't mean you're smart," Chris shot back at his twin.

"You think you're going to be able to get away with never cracking a book or studying for a test?" Ryan countered.

"Hey, my grades are okay," Chris said defensively. "But I've got better things to do than study . . ."

"Like play soccer?"

"Yeah, or baseball, or basketball . . ."

"You'll probably be the first high school freshman to become captain of the football team next year," Ryan sighed.

"That would be interesting, considering I don't play football," Chris pointed out.

"Oh, I'm sure they'll try to recruit you," Ryan predicted.

"You know you could play on all the teams I do, but you'd rather study," Chris said.

"And play in my younger brother's shadow?" Ryan replied. "No way. Besides, most girls are impressed by intelligence."

"Most teachers are, too. I can think of at least one who has a soft spot in her heart for Ryan here," a voice broke in. Ryan whirled around. Their friend Billy stood a few yards away, grinning widely, his auburn hair almost red in the bright sun.

"Who?" asked Ryan, his heart beating quickly.

Billy winked at Chris. "Why Mrs. Ziegler, our homeroom teacher. She's hot for smart boys like you."

"And I think Ryan has a crush on her, too," Chris added.

"I bet you'd make a good teacher's pet," Billy teased.

Ryan's face burned. "At least I don't fall in love with total bimbos like some people I know," he retaliated. "You've got a date with Vanna at seven-thirty every night, don't you Billy?"

"Never miss a night of the *Wheel* if I can help it," Billy replied.

"TV-brain," Ryan taunted.

"Anyway, I'll have to do without TV tonight," said Billy, "we're going to rough it and camp out under the stars. There's going to be a full moon, you know. I've staked out a great place near the woods, at the edge of the pasture, where we can sleep."

"A full moon? What'll we do about the werewolves?" Ryan asked impishly.

"Werewolves!" Billy's eyes lit up. "Will you tell stories like you did last time? Remember the one about the ax murderer? And you've got to make that great campfire stew. We can put Chris in charge of peeling potatoes."

"And what's your job going to be, Chief?" Chris asked.

"To enjoy myself, of course. You guys are lucky I'm not charging you to camp out on my property."

The twins cried out in outrage, and Billy turned to run for his life.

It had been a fun day, Ryan thought contentedly as he held out his stick toward the fire. Slowly, gently he turned it around, trying to get his marshmallow just the right shade of brown. Reaching for his soda, he took a swig. Ryan glanced over at his brother, who'd gone through almost an entire bag of marshmallows himself, and grimaced at the sticky black wad Chris was stuffing in his mouth. Billy burned his marshmallows as well—he was too impatient to take the time to brown them while Chris was too hungry to wait those few extra minutes. Ryan shook his head and concentrated on the task at hand. Easing his perfectly-browned marshmallows off the stick and onto a chocolate-covered graham cracker, he took a huge bite and stretched out his legs.

Through the trees Ryan could still see the setting sun, a sliver of orange red, the sky around it flooded with colors like pink, purple, and blue. Soon it would be dark, and the ritual storytelling would begin.

"Hey, look at Billy," Chris's voice interrupted his thoughts. Ryan glanced up and saw Billy standing, one hand holding a can of cola, the other pointing to a long line of spittle that was slowly descending from his mouth. Like a spider weaving its web, Billy's drool dropped down farther and farther, yet remained intact.

"What is he doing?" asked Ryan, caught somewhere between fascination and disgust.

"He's trying to get it to the ground without it breaking," said Chris watching, mesmerized.

"Are you sure he isn't cheating?" Ryan asked. "Is it part marshmallow taffy?"

"No, that's why he has the Coke—it makes your saliva sticky," Chris explained. "Haven't you seen the guys practicing at lunch?" Ryan shook his head. "Well, it's a real art," Chris continued. "Hah, it broke. Too bad, Billy."

Ryan rolled his eyes. "You guys are morons."

"I can't help it," said Billy. "It's the effect school has on me. It's harmful to my sanity."

"What sanity?" Chris snickered.

"Come on, you've got to admit it was a rough first month."

"The teachers are okay, but have you guys noticed how weird the girls are?" Chris ventured. "I don't understand what happened to them over the summer. Last year I was swimming and riding bikes with them, and now Wendy and Dede suddenly start giggling and blushing whenever I talk to them."

"They're admiring your muscles," Ryan commented dryly.

Chris gave Ryan a dirty look and turned to Billy. "And then at the swimming pool, this summer they'd come over and ask me for the time when the clock was right there in plain sight over the front desk."

"What are you complaining about? Send them over to me if you're not interested," Billy broke in.

"And what are *you* going to talk to them about?" Ryan asked.

"I'm not interested in *talking* to them," Billy snickered. "There are better things to do with girls."

"This guy's a real man of the world," Chris laughed.

"It's kind of a drag having to deal with girls and all, but it's not bad being the oldest in school," Ryan commented.

Billy nodded. "Yeah. We might as well enjoy it before we start high school next year." He raised his soda can. "Here's to our last year of junior high!"

"A toast," Chris said, lifting his can. "After all, I won't be captain of the soccer team next year. I might not even make varsity."

"Yeah, right. You'll probably have your letterman's jacket by the end of the year," Billy said.

"Billy, you could be one of the best players," Chris protested. "I don't know why you didn't go out for the team this fall."

For a moment Billy didn't respond. "Yeah, well my dad needs a lot of help working around the farm." Abruptly, he snapped his marsh-mallow stick in two and threw it down beside him. "It's not like he notices how hard I'm working to help him, though. Instead of thanking me, he tells me how I could've done it better. It doesn't matter to him if I have something to do after school."

"I bet he thinks it's great that you help him out," Ryan ventured.

"Oh, sure," Billy replied bitterly, "like you have to pry him away from me with a crowbar. He says good-bye every night after the chores are done, takes off for the local bar, and doesn't come back until after I'm sacked out."

Ryan glanced at his brother. He felt uncom-fortable, and didn't know what to say. He couldn't imagine what it would be like not to have his dad around. While George Taylor was a busy man and worked hard as city editor of Lakeview's daily newspaper, he always had time for them. Ryan was so used to sitting down to dinner every night in their red brick house on Sherman Avenue with both his parents, Chris and Lucy, his eight-year-old sister, that he couldn't imagine living any other way.

"Sounds like the next wild party should be at your house when you're dad's not around," Chris suggested, trying to make light of the situation.

But Billy didn't laugh or even crack a smile. He just kept rubbing the heel of his sneaker into the dirt. The twins looked at each other, and after a moment, Ryan leaned forward to begin his story, figuring now was as good a time as any for a distraction.

"Once upon a time," he began, "there was a family called the Smiths. One summer they held a big family reunion. Everyone was invited to the bash—grandparents, aunts, uncles, first and second cousins—which was held at the Smiths' summer house by Lake Watanabe, a place not too far from here, as a matter of fact." As he spoke, Ryan noticed, much to his relief, that Billy seemed to have relaxed a little.

"Mr. and Mrs. Smith, who were hosting the party, had two sons, Sam and Bart," Ryan continued. "These two brothers had grown up as best friends. Now that they were older, they worked in different cities, so they were especially excited to see each other again at the reunion. When Sam arrived, the first thing he did was look for Bart. But when he found him, he was disappointed to see that his brother had brought his new girlfriend, Maria. Sam figured they must be really serious, or his brother wouldn't have brought her. So he tried not to mind that he'd be spending less time alone with his brother and made an effort to be happy for them." Ryan paused to look over at Billy, who was slouched against a log with his eyes closed.

"Maria was fine at first," Ryan continued, concentrating his efforts on Chris, who listened expectantly. "But then she started acting weird. It all started when a long-lost cousin, Alfredo, showed up at the party."

"*Alfredo?* Are they an Italian family?" Billy snickered.

"Shhh, let him tell the story," Chris said.

"From the moment Alfredo arrived, Maria kept hanging around him, flirting, and you know, ignoring her date. She and Alfredo sat alone on the sofa, stared into each other's eyes and whispered—"

"Sweet nothings," Billy cackled.

"Do you want to tell the story yourself?" asked Ryan impatiently.

Billy waved his hand, dismissing Ryan's suggestion. "Go on," he grumbled.

"Because she was fooling around so much with Alfredo, Maria missed out on an important discussion with the rest of the family. Everyone had been talking about a wolf—at least that's what the people around Lake Watanabe thought it was— that had been roaming around the countryside at night, stealing chickens and attacking livestock. According to rumors, it was vicious and left strange marks on the animals. Worst of all, the wolf had almost eaten a human baby whose mother had left it on a screened-in porch while she was warming up a bottle in the kitchen.

The mother heard a growl and came back just in time to see this huge wolf-like creature chewing through the screen.

"But Maria didn't hear this, because she was so busy hanging out with Alfredo, bringing him plates of homemade fried chicken and glasses of lemonade. Alfredo seemed to be constantly thirsty and drank a lot."

"Those are signs of werewolves," Chris whispered to Billy. "They eat a lot of meat, and they're always thirsty."

"It was hard to imagine what Maria saw in Alfredo," Ryan continued patiently. "He was kind of funny looking. He had dark eyes and dark hair and his eyebrows met over his nose. He was so hairy that he even had little tufts growing on the palms of his hands. His eyes were so pale that he wore sunglasses all day long or the bright light would hurt them."

"That's another sign!" Chris cried.

"Anyhow, Maria didn't seem to mind any of this. She just kept on flirting, and Alfredo kept on encouraging her, and Bart just got madder and madder. Finally, Bart and Maria got in a fight after dinner. Sam was taking a walk down by the lake and that's how he overheard his brother and girlfriend arguing. After awhile, Maria apologized for her behavior, and they made up. Sam wasn't sure he trusted her though—after all, she was a girl— and so he went to bed still feeling uneasy about the whole thing. Because he was worried about his brother, he didn't sleep well that night.

"In the middle of night, Sam heard his brother moving around the room—he and Bart were sharing a bedroom. He opened his eyes and saw that Bart was staring out the window, muttering to himself. Sam crept up behind him and gasped when he saw what Bart was looking at.''

"I bet Maria and Alfredo were busy on the lawn together,'' Billy snickered, but he fell silent as Chris nudged him hard.

"It *was* Maria and Alfredo he was looking at,'' said Ryan. "They were holding hands and running toward the woods. When Bart saw them take off, he went berserk. Swearing he was going to kill Alfredo, he took off after them in a jealous rage. Sam was about to follow them when he heard a sound that made him stop in his tracks. He heard an eerie howling in the distance that sounded like a wild wolf! And his brother was running in that direction!''

"Sam figured that if wild wolves were going to attack, he needed help, so he woke up some of the guys and ordered them to bring sticks and clubs and knives—whatever they could find—and follow him.''

"I'd get my baseball bat,'' Billy said, beginning to look interested.

"How do you kill a werewolf?'' Chris couldn't help asking.

"If you let me finish the story, you'll find out!'' Ryan cried, taking a deep breath. "Sam and the other guys spread out. They figured they'd have a better chance of finding them that way. But as it turned out, Sam was the one who found all three.'' Ryan's voice dropped to a husky whisper. "He stumbled into a clearing and saw not one, but two wolflike creatures circling his brother. But before Sam could do anything, one of the werewolves attacked Bart and started to tear him limb from limb. There was blood everywhere! And Bart's cries were horrible—worse than what you'd hear in your worst nightmares! Then there was just a gurgling sound as the wolf sunk his teeth deep into Bart's throat.

"But Sam was brave and risked his life to save his brother. The other Smiths heard the commotion and ran through the woods to help. They came to the clearing just as Sam was strangling the wolf with his belt. The werewolf clawed at him and strained against the belt, his sharp fangs covered with blood and glistening in the moonlight, but finally Sam squeezed the last breath from the animal, and its dead body collapsed to the ground. As all the horrified Smiths watched, the wolf changed back to its human form, and Alfredo himself lay dead before them all.

"The other wolf had run howling off into the distance, but not before one of the Smith men had chopped off its left foot," Ryan explained. "When everyone got back to the house, carrying a wounded Bart and Alfredo's dead body, they found the woman Maria, lying in the yard. Although Bart was hurt, he was so relieved to see his girlfriend alive that he rushed over to where Maria lay. But when he got close, he screamed. Her left foot had been chopped off at the ankle! That's when they knew for sure that Alfredo had bitten her and turned Maria into the second werewolf!"

Chris and Billy shuddered. "Guess he broke up with her after that," Billy quipped. "Didn't he, Ryan?"

But Ryan only smiled. "They broke up that

night, but I'm not going to say they never got back together again. Whether Maria stayed a werewolf, or was cured or killed—that's another story."

Suddenly a blinding flash of light caused them to gasp. For a confused moment Ryan thought that someone had taken a picture of them before he realized it was lightning. In the next instant, Billy was on his feet.

"Did you see that animal?" he shouted. "Look over there toward the lake!"

"Where? What kind of animal?" Chris jumped up, looking wildly around him.

Before Billy could reply, a bone-chilling howl rang out, causing Ryan to scream in sheer terror. Turning their heads toward the sound, the boys saw the distant figure of a wolflike creature baring its fangs, illuminated by the next flash of lightning. The shock was so great that Ryan felt as if the breath had been knocked out of him.

"A werewolf!" Chris whispered.

Ryan shook his head. "No, it's impossible."

"You could have fooled me," Billy said.

"If this is a joke, Maguire, I don't think it's very funny!" Chris said threateningly, grabbing Billy's sleeve.

"You saw it! You heard the creature howl!" What do you think I did? Rigged up a light and sound show? You're crazy!" Billy yelled back, jerking his arm away from Chris. Then the tone of his voice changed. "What are you going to do now, sissies? Go crying home to your *mom* and tell her you're scared 'cause you saw a werewolf?" For a moment neither Chris nor Ryan spoke.

"I didn't say I was scared," Chris finally spoke up, trying to defend himself. "We were just trying to figure out what kind of animal that was. You have to admit it looked awfully like—"

"A werewolf," Billy finished for him. "So what if it is? What are we going to do about it?"

"We're going to sleep on it," Chris decided. "Maybe we can get a better look at him tomorrow morning when it's light."

"It'll be back in its human form then," Ryan reminded him.

Billy grinned as he knelt down to unzip his sleeping bag. "Pleasant dreams, guys. I guess we should have rented a movie and stayed over at your house."

TWO

Spiders.

Big, black hairy spiders were crawling all over his face: *Get them off!*

Ryan sat up abruptly, clawing his face with his hands. He was gasping for breath. But it wasn't spiders. Rain was falling on his face! He glanced around quickly—it was pitch black and pouring.

"Thunderstorm!" he cried out, but Chris and Billy were already up, cursing in the darkness as they stumbled over their sleeping bags and groped around the wet ground for the flashlight. Ryan pulled on his sneakers, fished out the flashlight he'd brought from his pack and was up in a flash.

Billy stubbed his toe on a damp log, then crashed into Chris, who was crawling along the ground. Cursing the wind, the rain, the twins and his rotten luck, Billy finally succeeded in scooping up his belongings and running over to where Ryan stood.

"You got everything?" Ryan asked, sweeping campsite with his light.

16

"Yeah," said Billy. "And here comes Chris."

"Which way is your house?" Ryan asked. "I can't see a thing!"

"Shine it this way. That's right. Let's go. No, not over there—here, this way!" Billy directed impatiently.

"Wait for me!" Chris called, his voice almost lost in the wind.

"Hold the flashlight steady up there! I can't see!" Billy yelled at Ryan as they ran. Laughing and shouting at each other, the threesome raced through the woods and the underbrush, back out into a field.

"This way!" shouted Billy.

"But your house is up over this hill!" Ryan cried.

"Come on, you wimps, we're not going back to my house!" Billy said.

"You have a better idea?" coughed Chris, shivering as the cold water ran down his neck.

"Yeah, turn right here and we'll spend the night in the hay barn. It'll be real cozy. We just fixed the roof, and it's a lot closer than the house." In the fraction of a second that the twins hesitated, an unearthly howl sounded in the distance. Grabbing the flashlight, Billy took the lead.

Running blindly behind him through the wet night, Chris and Ryan followed, stumbling over branches and clumps of grass. Finally, just as Ryan felt his arms begin to give out under the weight of the packs, bags, and clothes he was carrying, he saw Billing gesturing wildly.

"There's the barn! See it?" he shouted hoarsely. Sloshing through the mud up to the wooden building, Billy pulled open the heavy sliding door. The three of them squeezed in, and the twins found themselves standing inside the old barn. Billy shone the flashlight beam around, searching the pitch black interior.

Is he looking for a light switch? Ryan wondered. The scent of fresh hay filled the damp night air, and the tinny sound of rain falling on the newly mended roof made him feel glad they'd found shelter at last. But something felt wrong and he wasn't able to relax. *Something evil was here in the barn.* But that was silly, Ryan told himself. He'd been in this barn a dozen times before in the daytime. Remembering the swing they'd rigged up to the rafters above during the summer, Ryan tried to recapture happy memories of being there in the daylight. Instead, goosebumps rose on his arms and legs, and he shivered.

Finally Billy managed to find a string and tugged on it turning on a single dust-covered light bulb. Dim light flooded the barn, but above in the loft, deep black shadows remained. *Anything or anyone could be hiding in this hay*, Ryan thought, his mouth dry. With his flashlight, he tried to make out shapes in the shadows. For a moment Ryan thought he saw something move, and he took a step backward.

Ryan screamed as the hairy arm of a werewolf brushed against his neck.

With a startled cry, Chris whirled around to face his brother. But the fear on his face turned to amusement when he saw what his twin had backed up against.

"What the heck is the matter with you?" cried

Billy, stomping indignantly through the hay toward Ryan. "Cripes! Since when does an old rope swing scare you?" He fingered the frayed and knotted rope they'd fastened to the rafter above only a few short months ago. "Don't you remember when we rigged this up last June?"

Ryan took a deep breath. "Yeah, sure I do. It's just that the rope felt like a hairy . . . Hey, I'm sorry, you guys, I just got spooked, that's all."

"If you scream like that again, you really will wake a werewolf," Chris said, keeping his voice steady to disguise the fact that he, too, was feeling strangely uncomfortable in the dark barn. "Maybe you should quit making up those stories."

Ryan shrugged, hoping he didn't look as embarrassed as he felt. "All right, all right, let's throw down our bags and get back to sleep. You can give me more grief in the morning." Dropping his sleeping bag beside a bale of hay, Ryan sank wearily to the ground and pulled off his running shoes. He peeled off his jacket, and began stuffing it with hay to make a pillow for himself. But as he reached for another fistful, he felt his hand touch something cold and metallic. His fingers closed around the object. When he held it up in the dim light, all three boys gasped.

It was a knife. The four-inch blade, caked with grime and encrusted with a reddish substance, looked menacing in the semidarkness.

For a moment no one said anything. "This belong to you, Billy?" Ryan finally whispered.

Fascinated, Billy reached out his hand to examine the deadly weapon. When Billy turned the knife over, he gave a nod of recognition.

Fitting the blade back into the black rubber sheath, he said, "It's not mine, but I recognize the make. It's a Kershaw Black Horse. I was going to ask for one for my birthday—for cleaning fish. It's a serious knife, not half- gadget, half-toy like some of those little Swiss Army models. I wonder what it's doing here?"

"And why did we find it with the blade pulled out?" Chris whispered.

"Look at this stuff. Do you think it's blood?" Ryan asked, examining the blade more closely.

"It's hard to tell in this light," Billy replied.

"Who could it belong to?" Chris asked, his voice cracking a bit. "How long do you think it's been here?"

"Probably about as long as the ax murderer who owns it has been living in my barn," Billy replied cheerfully.

"It's a knife, not an ax, so he can't be an ax murderer," Chris pointed out disgustedly.

"Maybe he left his ax at home," Billy teased. "Come on you guys, we're not worth killing, and there's nothing here to steal."

"Yeah," Chris said, feeling the tension leave his shoulders, "you're right, Billy."

Ryan said nothing. Billy was being reasonable, but he couldn't help but feel there was more to finding the knife than anyone was willing to admit. And he couldn't forget that creepy sensation that had haunted him ever since they'd walked through the barn door.

"I don't think this is anything to joke about," Ryan spoke up. "A normal person wouldn't carry around a knife with dried blood on it. This weapon could belong to some crazy who's escaped from the loony bin—you know the state mental institution's only an hour away. The blood could be from a farm chicken he's killed for food," Ryan paused dramatically, "or it could be from someone . . ."

"Gee, I never thought of that. Maybe we *should* call the police," Billy said. "And just to show you what a great guy I am, I'll let you do all the talking when the cops come. Go for it, Ryan. Tell them we've got us a psychopath here." Billy paused, and looked slyly over at Chris. "But, uh, don't count on Chris and me to back you up. We'll be up at the lake tomorrow morning catching fish."

Ryan was speechless, too angry to say anything. He wished he were camping out alone with his brother. Instead, they were stuck with this lardball. Why was Billy so obnoxious? Why did he have to tag around with them all the time? Last week alone, Billy had eaten dinner at the Taylors' house two nights in a row! What was he trying to do? And what really got on Ryan's nerves was that Chris seemed to go along with whatever Billy said.

"Give me a break," Ryan mumbled, turning away.

Chris's smile quickly faded, and he felt guilty as he realized that Ryan was upset. Why, he wondered, did he always feel stuck in the middle, torn between his brother and his best friend? Why couldn't they get along better? Of course Billy's jokes did get out of hand sometimes, but why couldn't Ryan realize that his jokes weren't meant to be mean. And tonight Billy was just trying to lighten up a grim situation.

Chris wondered if he should tell Billy to lay off Ryan for awhile. The trouble was, he didn't like to criticize Billy, who had troubles at home. His father drank a lot, and he didn't have a mom, at least not anymore. Mrs. Maguire had left when Billy was only six years old. She never came back or even wrote a letter, which Chris found especially hard to believe. Billy almost never talked about his mom, although once he had told Chris that if he ever got rich, he was going to hire a private investigator to track her down. Chris had seen a photograph of her once on Billy's dresser. The family was dressed up, and Mrs. Maguire was smiling and holding Billy's hand. He glanced over at his brother and saw that Ryan was still scowling.

"Come on, big brother, Billy's only kidding around," Chris said. "We're all getting too uptight. Finding the knife is no big deal. Some apple picker probably dropped it. You know we'll never find any real danger here in Lakeview. This town is the most boring place I know."

Ryan nodded. "I don't understand why I'm so jumpy. It's just that I know something's wrong." He leaned back against the wooden wall of the barn. "Sometimes I get these feelings," Ryan tried to explain, struggling for words, "like now, I think . . ."

"I think you're probably hungry." Chris said quickly, not wanting to hear what Ryan had to say. Pulling a package of chocolate cupcakes from out of his backpack, he grinned. "Anyone care to join me for a midnight snack?"

Ryan gave up. He *was* hungry, and maybe he'd feel less anxious in the morning.

* * *

"I guess we're not fishing today," Chris said gloomily as they stared out the barn door at the gray drizzle the next morning. Putting on his Royals cap, he looked over at Billy. "Or are we?"

Billy shrugged. "Rain doesn't bother the fish— they'll bite anyway." He paused, then added, "But let's talk about it over pancakes." He looked over at Ryan. "How about it, Chef?"

As they took off for the house Chris saw the sickening sight first, and he sprang backwards. He felt nauseated as he stared down at the dead squirrel, realizing he'd almost stepped on it.

"Ryan! Billy!" His voice was shaking as he stared at the bloody corpse lying in the road.

Ryan came running up. "What is it?" Then he stopped short. "Oh, no."

"I don't think it's been dead too long," Chris said, pulling off his baseball cap and twisting it nervously in his hands. There was a faint trail of blood leading from the grass onto the dirt road where it had collapsed.

"Is that a squirrel, or did someone break a jar of tomato sauce?" Billy asked, coming up behind them.

Chris didn't bother to reply—Billy's remark just wasn't very funny. "It's been chewed up pretty good. Look at those teeth marks," he said, pointing with an unsteady hand.

"Is that what those huge gashes are from?" Ryan asked.

"I think so," Chris said.

"What could have done that?" Ryan asked, "except—"

"Some sort of horrible beast," Chris continued, looking expectantly at his brother.

"Like a werewolf?" Ryan said faintly, trying not to look at the mangled squirrel. He remembered the howling that had awakened him shortly after they'd fallen asleep in the barn.

"Come on, you guys," Billy said gruffly. "Animals fight and get killed all the time. What are you making such a big deal about this?" He turned and headed downhill to the tool shed, returning a few minutes later with a shovel. "We'd better bury the poor sucker before he's covered with maggots."

"I . . . don't . . . think . . . I can," said Ryan. His stomach felt funny all of a sudden, and he sat down in the dirt so he wouldn't faint. Visions of werewolf jaws sinking into a furry squirrel swam before his eyes. He watched silently as his brother and Billy hurriedly dug a grave just off the road. "I saw this movie once about a kid who had this weird power," Ryan told them. "Everything he made up became real." He paused. "Do you think the werewolf from my story has come to life?"

"Cut it out!" Billy said. His shovel hit a rock embedded in the damp earth and he swore out loud, then he determinedly scooped up the dead creature with his shovel. He brought it over to the hole he and Chris had dug and dumped it in. "It was definitely killed by an animal. Those aren't clean knife wounds," he said. "Now come on. Let's go eat breakfast."

"Eat breakfast?" Ryan echoed in disbelief.

"You bet," said Billy, leading the way up to his house.

"I can hardly wait," Chris said enthusiastically. "Bacon, pancakes, orange juice . . ."

"What would you guys do if I weren't here to do the cooking?" Ryan grumbled.

The boys fell silent as they entered the kitchen and saw Billy's father sitting at the table. Mr. Maguire looked a little pale and was resting his forehead in his hands. Chris looked at Billy's worried face and felt a rush of sympathy, hoping that Mr. Maguire wouldn't be too hung over. It was impossible to tell what kind of mood he'd be in after a Saturday night of drinking.

Mr. Maguire looked at them, his face completely blank. Then suddenly, he broke into a smile. "Mind if I join you boys for breakfast?"

"That would be great, Dad," Billy said eagerly, the tension broken. "Ryan makes the best pancakes in the world."

"I'd appreciate that," replied his father. "I just went down to the chicken coop to collect eggs and discovered that we've had a break in."

"What did you find?" Billy asked.

"Some wild animal got into the chicken coup last night and made off with one of our birds. I suppose I should be glad he only made off with one," Mr. Maguire continued, "but the rest are scared to death, clucking away, and not laying like they should be. The animal must've been pretty strong to jump over the fence like it did and then jump over it again to get out, with a squawking chicken in its mouth."

"What do you think it could be, Dad?" Billy asked as he gave Chris and Ryan a knowing look.

"Could be a fox, I don't know. I didn't think there were any around here. The trouble is," said

Mr. Maguire, "there's no guarantee the animal won't come back and get another chicken tonight unless I figure out a way to protect them. Was it wet enough for you kids out there last night?"

"We moved to the barn when the rain started," Chris explained.

"I'm glad you boys found it before you got too soaked. We don't use the old barn anymore except to store extra hay there for Sam Pearson's horses. You know he bought the old Wilson farm next door?" Chris looked nervously at Ryan as Mr. Maguire rambled on. It was as if Billy's father had forgotten they were there. "Funny fellow. Never farmed before, but he said he was going to start up a riding stable, and he does have some horses. Pearson moved here last year from Kansas City. He paid Wilson's asking price for the farm in cash and has pretty much stuck to himself ever since. Has a pretty new wife, though, I hear."

"So how are the Raiders doing this year?" Mr. Maguire asked, abruptly changing the subject. "Billy says you're the star of the soccer team, Chris."

Chris grinned, only too happy launch into stories about the team.

How does Chris do it? Ryan marveled, as he listened to his brother and Mr. Maguire discuss the Marshall Junior High soccer team. Chris could get along with anybody. Mr. Maguire was normally a taciturn man, but here was Chris, shooting the breeze with him.

Ryan remembered how on their ninth birthday his twin had insisted on inviting their entire class to their birthday party—even fat Bernie Baker, who was considered a loser. At the party, when Bernie arrived, Chris went right up to him, slung an arm around him, and said how glad he was that Bernie could come. Ryan had never forgotten that.

Chris looked up and realized that Billy was standing dejectedly at the sink. "Hey Billy," he said quickly, "tell your dad what we found."

"Um, Dad, we found a pocket knife in the barn last night, a really cool one," Billy began, extracting the shiny instrument from his back pocket and handing it to his father. "How do you think it got there?"

His father looked at it only a moment before replying. "Pearson or someone in his crew probably dropped the knife when the hay was delivered. I suppose I should give him a call and ask him. And, of course, we've had apple pickers traipsing around the property these last few months. One of them could have wandered over to the barn and lost it there. Shouldn't have been in there, but I can't keep track of everyone. We need a large crew to work the trees; all the fruit gets ripe at once. That reminds me, Billy, I need you to man the cash register today down at the shop. Lots of people been coming to get apples and cider these past few weekends. In fact," he looked at his watch, "I'm on my way down to the orchard now. Join me there in half an hour," he said, standing up abruptly, breakfast forgotten.

Billy was quiet for a moment. "Yeah, I'll be there," he mumbled under his breath. After his father had gone, he turned to the twins. "See you guys later. Have fun—whatever you end up doing," he said dejectedly.

"We were just going to sit around today anyway. You're not missing out," Chris said as he and Ryan followed Billy outside. "Listen, I left the backpack with all our food in the barn. We'll walk you part of the way to the orchard."

"Okay," said Billy tonelessly, leading them to the barn. But when they got there, Chris's backpack was not to be found.

"This is weird," Chris said in a tight voice as he searched the dim interior. "Something is going on here. I know where I left the pack."

Billy looked impatiently at his watch, obviously anxious to leave. "Listen, I've got to go meet my dad. You guys can stay here and keep looking. It's probably buried in the hay somewhere."

"I'll talk to you later," Chris called over his shoulder as Billy took off down the hill to the orchard shop.

"We'd better go, Chris," Ryan said, glad to have an excuse to leave the barn, which was starting to feel like a really creepy place. "It's barely drizzling now, so it's a good time to ride home. It'll be raining harder in a little while."

Chris shrugged and left the barn with Ryan following closely behind. Ryan turned to slide the heavy door shut, when he heard a noise inside the barn.

"Come on, our bikes are up at the house. I'll race you there," challenged Chris.

"No, wait a minute. I heard something move in the barn," Ryan said in a low voice. "A kind of rustling sound."

Chris turned around. "Should we go back in?"

"I guess," Ryan said hesitantly. "Maybe just one of us should go."

"I'll flip you for it," Chris said, pulling out a quarter from his pocket. Chris flipped the coin, and grinned triumphantly at his twin.

"Darn!" Ryan swore under his breath as he squeezed through the barn door and stood alone in the gloom. *I can't believe I'm sneaking around Billy's barn looking for monsters or whatever else might be hiding in here*, he thought as he crept around. As his eyes adjusted to the light, he glanced around nervously. He couldn't leave now—Chris was outside, and there was no way he'd let his brother think he was a coward.

Besides, it was his own fault for even mentioning the noise. He could have just kept quiet and headed back home with Chris.

For a second Ryan thought he was going to sneeze. Then he rubbed a finger under his nose, just as Chris had taught him, and the urge disappeared. Stepping through the loose hay strewn across the wooden floor, Ryan tried to be careful, willing himself not to step on squeaky boards. Stealthily he made his way around the inside of the barn, poking into corners and scrutinizing every little pile of hay for a carelessly uncovered foot or finger . . . or paw.

The air smelled musty and damp, reminding him of the way a dog smelled after coming in out of the rain. Ryan wished he had a dog with him now, who would stay by his side and protect him. *Come on, you're almost finished*, he told himself. He'd made his way around the entire perimeter of the ground floor. Now all he had to do was climb the ladder and check the loft.

Ryan licked his lips nervously as he stared up the ladder to the loft above. *One step at a time*, he thought, beginning to climb. He reached the top and looked around. No sign of life—or death for that matter. The roof slanted down toward the platform floor so it was quite dark in the corners where they met, but there really wasn't much space in which to hide. He could see the whole floor—there was no one up there. Ryan heaved a sigh of relief and began to climb back down the ladder.

Just then, Ryan heard a rustling noise and froze in midstep. Someone or something was moving in the hay down below. But hadn't he searched everywhere? Ryan groaned.

He waited, listening for the rustling sound again, but it had stopped. Then without warning it started again, sounding fainter this time. What could it be? he wondered. All at once anger erupted inside him. Chris and Billy had set him up! They were hiding somewhere down there, making the noise themselves and laughing their heads off at him. Worst of all, he deserved it because he was the world's biggest sucker.

Ryan descended the ladder with lightning speed and he stormed angrily across the barn. Hesitating for just a moment before peering past a tall bale of hay that stood in a corner, he saw nothing in the dark at first, then he heard a low, throaty growl and a black shape rose up before him.

THREE

Ryan stared at a pair of sharp, pointed ears and saw a flash of white teeth, as the creature's black lips curled back in surprise and fear. Then the black Labrador sprang past him, knocking Ryan down as he raced around the barn, barking and howling. Scrambling to his feet, Ryan watched as the dog ran to the other end of the barn and cowered in the corner. *A dog!* he thought, starting to laugh with relief. It was only a black Labrador retriever. No wonder they had heard howling in the night! The poor thing looked mangy and was obviously half-starved.

"Ryan! Ryan! Are you okay?" Chris shouted hoarsely, bursting through the door. "I heard you shout and—"

"Shhhhh. Don't scare him anymore than he already is," Ryan cautioned, pointing toward the dog.

When Chris saw the animal, his face lit up with delight. "A black Lab! Where did you find him?" he cried. "He must be a stray. Oh, and what a beauty he could be, too, if he were well fed. Hey

31

there, fella," Chris coaxed the dog, walking slowly toward it. "Good boy. I'm not going to hurt you. I want to be your friend. I bet you're hungry, and guess what? I have something for you to eat." Pulling out a few cookies from his jacket pocket, Chris extended his hand, placing one cookie on the ground in front of the animal. Continuing to talk, Chris offered another cookie after the dog gobbled up the first one.

The dog looked up at Chris expectantly, then began to lick his fingers. His heart pounding excitedly, Chris sat back on his heels. If only he and Ryan could keep him! The dog didn't have a collar and, judging from his condition, he obviously didn't belong to anybody. And he and Ryan and Lucy had always wanted a pet . . .

"He's wonderful," Chris declared, feeding the Lab his last cookie and scratching his ears.

"How do you know he's not a she?" Ryan asked, coming closer.

"I don't. She's wonderful, too—if that's what she is," Chris responded happily.

"What should we call her?" Ryan asked, assuming that Chris felt the same way he did about keeping the dog.

"Good question," Chris said. "Just don't let Lucy do it. She'll name it after one of those rock stars she's so crazy about."

"Well, Prince wouldn't be such a bad name," Ryan quipped, and his brother laughed. "I just hope Mom lets us keep him considering . . ."

Chris jumped up in alarm. "If you sneeze once in front of Mom, and we have to get rid of him because of your dumb allergies, I'll kill you!" he threatened.

"It's not just me. I'm not the only one with allergies!" Ryan defended himself. "Dad has them too!"

"But he's mostly allergic to cats. I don't care about cats. I want to keep this dog!" Chris threw his arms around the Lab and frowned up at his twin.

"Hey, I feel the same way!" Ryan said. "I won't let Mom send him away."

"He looks like a full-blooded Labrador retriever, and they're worth some money you know," Chris pointed out. "Maybe we can appeal to Mom's practical side and tell her he'd be a good investment."

"You want to fatten him up and then sell him for a profit?" Ryan teased. "Anyway, it looks like our werewolf mystery is solved. This fella looks hungry enough to have attacked that squirrel and I'm sure he was the one howling during the lightning last night."

Chris nodded. "Makes sense. I bet the Lab broke into the Maguires' poultry house and stole that chicken, too. Do you think he'll follow us home, Ryan?"

"If you keep feeding him, he sure will."

"We'll have to go borrow some food from Billy's kitchen, but I bet if we ride real slow—"

Ryan snapped his fingers. "I've got it! We'll call him Alfredo." He looked at Chris's face. "After the werewolf in my story, you know?"

"Alfredo wouldn't be my first choice." Chris began.

"We can call him Fred for short," Ryan compromised.

"Deal," Chris said. Turning to the Lab, he

whistled. "C'mon, boy. C'mon, Fred. We're taking you home!"

"Gross! What happened to you? You're all wet and muddy!" Lucy said, scrunching up her nose in distaste, as the back door flew open and Chris hurried into the kitchen.

Chris stared at his sister. Lucy's short blond curls seemed charged with electricity this morning, flying out wildly in all directions as she sat at the table, painting bright pink polish on her nails. Lucy sat cross-legged on a chair, wrapped in her favorite fuzzy pink bathrobe. Strewn across the breakfast table before her lay half-empty Chinese food cartons.

"Lucy, what's really yucky is eating leftover Chinese food for breakfast," Chris countered. "What did you do—put your finger in a socket this morning?"

"Ha, ha. You're so out of it, you can't even appreciate the latest hairstyle. Sally Ward slept over last night. We did each other's hair—this is the latest style from *Seventeen* magazine. And I'll bet you never tried Chinese food in the morning. Besides," Lucy added, sticking out her lower lip in a pout, "Ryan wasn't here to cook pancakes, so I had to eat something."

"Where's Sally?" Chris asked, scraping some Moo Shu Pork onto a plate.

"She had to go somewhere with her parents."

"Why didn't Mom or Dad make breakfast for you?"

"Mom had to leave early to show houses, and Dad's at the paper. What makes you think I'd eat anything Dad cooked anyway?" Lucy watched her brother with interest. "So you're going to try Chinese food for breakfast after all?"

"I'm not," Chris said, picking up the dish, "but Fred is."

A loud bark came at the door. Twisting around in her seat, Lucy saw the large black dog on the other side of the screen and screamed with delight.

"It's okay, Ryan," Chris called out. "Mom and Dad aren't home."

As Ryan opened the screen door, Fred trotted up to Lucy, and began wagging his tail furiously, eager to play. Chris set down the plate of Chinese food and, after a few tentative licks, the Lab began to eat heartily.

"He's the most beautiful dog I've ever seen. Will Mom let us keep him?" Lucy squealed.

"Maybe," Chris ventured, "if we went to the store and bought food and dog biscuits and everything Fred'll need with our allowances . . ."

"It might be easier for Mom and Dad to accept him." Ryan finished for him. "It'll look like everything's already been decided on and taken care of."

"They won't need to do a thing." Chris agreed. He turned back to his sister. "When's Dad getting home?"

"Around noon. He needs a bath," Lucy said.

"Dad does?" Chris asked, confused.

"No, the dog. Look how dirty my hands are from petting him."

"Okay, that'll be our project for the afternoon," Chris told her. "I'll go to the store for supplies. You'd better come too, big brother, or I won't be able to carry it all."

"Where's Billy?" Lucy asked.

Chris looked at Ryan and tried not to laugh. His little sister had a gigantic crush on Billy, and they both thought it was hilarious, though Ryan always begged him not to tease her. But Chris couldn't help it—it was great fun to watch Billy fend off her flirting.

"Billy had to work on the farm today," Ryan said. Lucy's face fell. "But, uh, he told us to say 'hi' to you."

"Oh good," Lucy said, smiling broadly. "When's he coming over again?"

"Lucy, you have your own friends, you know," Chris said.

"Yeah, but they can't always come over, and Mom can't drive me anywhere because she's always working," Lucy said, beginning to whine.

Ryan sighed. He wished his mom were around more, too. Taking on many of the chores she'd done in the past was no fun—things like helping Lucy with her homework and cooking meals for the rest of the family. The trouble was, he reflected, they'd all been spoiled. Up until last spring, their mother had stayed at home. She'd been a traditional cookie-baking, carpooling, full-time mother. Then out of the blue, or so it had seemed to all of them, she decided to become Phyllis Taylor, real estate agent.

"Think about the good side to her being gone," Ryan suggested, noticing that Lucy still looked downcast.

"What's that?" Lucy asked suspiciously.

"Think of all the pizza and Chinese food we've ordered out for in the last month," Ryan said. "And since I'm sure Mom feels guilty about

leaving you alone in the afternoons, she'll probably let us keep Fred!"

"We'd better go if we want to get to the store
before they come home," Chris said, looking at
his watch.

"Okay," Ryan said. "Lucy, don't let Fred out
of the kitchen. He might make a mess in the
house, and then Mom will never let us keep
him." He turned back to Chris. "I'm going to go
get another backpack. I'll meet you out front
where we left the bikes."

"Sit, Fred," said Lucy as he left the room.
"Beg. Heel. Roll over. Bark."

"Teach him one thing at a time, Lucy!" Ryan
called out, chuckling to himself as he ran up the
stairs.

FOUR

"Here comes the rain!" Chris cried.

"We made it to the store just in time!" Ryan replied. Both boys swerved to the right, riding up over the curb and coasting into the convenience store parking lot. Chris hopped off his bike and hurried into the store. Ryan, as usual, stayed behind to lock the bikes together. Ignoring the chilly drops that streamed down his neck, he quickly wound the metal chain through the spokes of their wheels.

As Ryan darted through the door, he saw that Chris was standing by the checkout counter, holding a box of doughnuts and talking to Jack Moses, a guy who'd been on the soccer team with Chris last year. His brother was nodding sympathetically, listening to some kind of story that Jack was telling him. As Ryan walked up to them, he noticed that Jack was pouring out two cups of steaming hot cocoa. The rich aroma made his stomach rumble.

"Hi Jack, how're you doing?" Ryan said, accepting a cup. "How's high school?"

"Not too bad. That is, if you don't mind being dumped on by the creeps who call themselves upperclassmen," Jack replied.

"It's tough being the youngest?" Ryan asked.

"Yeah," Jack complained. "My buddy Pete was actually folded up and locked in his locker the other day," Jack told them.

"I can't believe Pete would fit into a locker!" Chris exclaimed, horrified.

"Yeah, I know. A teacher heard him screaming, opened up the locker, and he fell out. It took awhile for Pete to get the feeling back in his legs," Jack said.

"Guess we'd better have fun this year," Chris said, quickly downing his hot chocolate.

Jack glanced around nervously. "I wish I could talk to you guys for awhile, but I can't." He turned to Ryan. "I was just telling Chris that my manager's really mad at me. While we were taking inventory this morning, he discovered some food and alcohol are missing, and now he's blaming it on me. I work here weekends, and my friends usually come by to hang around for awhile and talk to me. No big deal, right? Wrong. My boss thinks they're stealing stuff." Jack banged his fist on the counter. "It's so unfair. I know my buddies didn't take anything, and I would never steal from the store. This job is way too important to me."

"Who do you think did it then?" Ryan asked.

"I think it was this weird guy who came into the shop yesterday," Jack replied.

"Weird? In what way?" Ryan asked.

"What did he look like?" Chris persisted.

"He was middle-aged, and tall with really

short, almost shaved dark hair. And he had a lot
of stubble on his face. Basically he looked scuzzy,
like the kind of guy who'd steal whiskey. He
wore a blue shirt—that's about all I remember."

"Was he a bag man?" Ryan asked.

"No, he wasn't crazy at all. He was definitely
all there. But his eyes were . . ." Jack paused,
"hostile. He gave me the creeps, so finally I asked
if I could help him with something. He said no
and then a group of people came in and after I
finished ringing up their stuff, the guy was
gone."

"Did he ever come back?" Ryan asked,
helping himself to another doughnut before Chris
could finish off the box.

Jack nodded. "Yeah, the next time he bought
a cup of coffee and stood around looking at
magazines. Then some friends of mine distracted
me. When I looked up again, he was gone. I think
that's when the stuff disappeared."

"How much is missing?" Ryan asked.

"A couple of bottles of whiskey and some dry
goods," Jack answered.

"He could have carried that out in two trips,"
Ryan figured.

"Sure could," Jack told him. "The trouble is,
my boss doesn't even believe this man exists." At
that moment an older, grumpy-looking man
poked his head out of a back room. His scowl
deepened when he saw the twins.

"Jack," he said in a warning tone.

"I'll go get the dog food," Ryan offered.

"Down aisle four," Jack pointed out.

Chris waved. "Hello, sir," he said in his friendliest manner. The manager ignored Chris and ducked back into his office.

Rolling his eyes, Jack rang up their purchases. "Have fun with your new dog," he said to the twins, handing over their bags.

"Don't let the big boys push you around at school," Chris winked at him as they headed for the exit.

"Darn it. The rain's really coming down now," Ryan observed when they got to the door.

Chris put down his bag. "Let's look at magazines for awhile then," he suggested, picking up a copy of *Sports Illustrated*.

Ryan began leafing through the rack, looking for a copy of *Popular Photography* when suddenly a headline caught his eye from the front page of the Sunday *Tribune*:

Convict Escapes From Federal Penitentiary

"Look at this, Chris," Ryan whispered excitedly, grabbing his brother's arm.

Lakeview, Kansas—Joe Hoffman, who is serving a twenty-five-year sentence for armed robbery and attempted murder, made a dramatic and daring escape from the federal penitentiary in Lawrenceville on Friday afternoon. Hoffman, who was recently denied parole after a five-year review, escaped after fatally stabbing a prison guard.

Ryan looked up at his brother. "Are you thinking what I'm thinking? The dried blood on the knife we found. It could have been from the prison guard he attacked!" Ryan whispered.

"You know we never did find my backpack,"

Chris said, staring at Hoffman's photo. "It would be a mighty nice pack for someone traveling on foot to have . . . Hey, look at this! They're offering a five-thousand dollar reward to anyone who can find him! Think of the sports equipment that could buy! And there'd be enough left over for you to get a new camera. It says here they think he's headed for Kansas City. Lakeview is right on the way!" Chris looked up at his twin. "Ryan, I bet the knife we found belongs to Joe Hoffman. I'll bet he was right there in the barn with us!"

"But I searched the barn! No one was there except for Fred," Ryan protested.

"So? That was this morning. Hoffman could've snuck out last night after we'd gone to sleep. That's probably when he took the pack. Fred could've snuck into the barn while we ate breakfast at the house," Chris reasoned.

"But why wouldn't Hoffman have taken his knife with him?" Ryan challenged his brother.

"Because Billy was sleeping on it!" Chris reminded him. "Don't you remember?" Chris clenched his fists excitedly. "I can't believe it, but what you said about an escaped lunatic is probably true! Only an escaped murderer is even better!"

"Are you missing a screw or something?" Ryan said. "We don't have any evidence that Hoffman was hiding out on the farm." But even as he spoke, Ryan remembered the feeling of fear that engulfed him when he walked into the barn. What if Hoffman really had been hiding there? "Listen, let's stay calm," he said, starting to panic.

"Stay calm? Hah! This is the most exciting thing that's ever happened to us! What are we waiting for? Let's go back to the farm and capture him!" Chris cried. "Aren't you excited about the money? We could get Mom to stop selling houses and start baking chocolate chip cookies again."

Ryan laughed. "I doubt it. Look, the rain has let up. Let's go home and talk to Dad about this. Since he works at the *Tribune*, he may know something we don't."

"If you're afraid, I'll go back by myself and get Billy. He'll look for Hoffman with me," Chris said.

"Listen," Ryan hissed, taking Chris by the arm and dragging him outside. "If Hoffman was hiding out in the barn, he's probably long gone by now."

"But—"

"You don't know what you're doing. This guy is obviously very dangerous—he could kill us! Let's talk to Dad about this first. He may have more information about this case than the article reveals. We'll tell him what happened, then he can help us decide what to do. You still might have a chance to go back to the farm and see some action, okay?"

Angrily Chris pulled his arm away. "Okay," he said sullenly. What a pain his common sense, stick-in-the-mud brother was getting to be! Ryan was too worried about getting into trouble, he thought resentfully, too concerned about playing it safe. If he always did what Ryan told him to do, he'd never have any fun. Well, if he was ever going to have a real adventure, he'd probably have to do it without his twin. This escaped convict thing sounded promising. He'd call Billy when they got home, and together they'd plan something. *Without telling any adults*, he decided as he stood waiting for his twin to unlock their bikes. *And maybe without telling Ryan.*

FIVE

Later that afternoon, Ryan heard the front door shut from upstairs in his bedroom. Was Chris back already from walking Fred? he wondered.

"Anybody home?" his father called.

Ryan jumped up from the floor where he was putting together a portfolio of his best photographs and hurried to the stairs. As he passed his parents' bedroom he glimpsed Lucy on the phone inside and sighed with relief. Now he'd be able to catch some time alone with his dad to tell him about Fred. And about Joe Hoffman.

His father stood in the hallway, taking off his overcoat. Wearing his traditional rumpled, white cotton shirt with his necktie askew and a pair of tortoiseshell glasses, George Taylor looked thoroughly disheveled. Ryan could just imagine his father running out of the house early that morning—grabbing his old brown cardigan sweater and pulling on a pair of mismatched socks and downing a mug of black coffee—oblivious to everything but the breaking story at hand.

"Hi, Dad," Ryan said. "What were you doing at the office today? Don't editors get Sunday off like other people?"

George Taylor smiled at his son. "I'm working on a hot story. It'll all be worth it when they hand me the Pulitzer Prize," he joked. Then in spite of himself, he yawned, stretching his long arms over his head. Mr. Taylor was a large man, not heavy, but very tall. As Ryan watched him, he wished for the hundredth time that he, and not Chris, had inherited his father's solid build.

Ryan cleared his throat. "Could I talk to you about something? It's kind of important."

George Taylor nodded his head. "Sure, son. Let's go down to my study. I wanted to put in a few hours of work on my novel before dinner. I can't believe it's already three o'clock."

They started down the steps to the basement, the area Ryan's father liked to call his study. The truth was, his study was only one corner of the damp basement where he kept his computer and research files. On weekends and sometimes late at night, George Taylor worked on his crime novel. He'd been writing it for years, but he was very secretive about it, and no one in the family had ever read it.

"You killed anybody off yet?" Ryan asked, knowing *he* would kill to see so much as a single chapter.

His father smiled enigmatically. "You'll have to wait and see."

Chris walked at a leisurely pace back to the house. He wore his Walkman headphones to stay tuned into a Kansas City Chiefs football game on the radio while he kept an eye on Fred. But he wasn't really thinking about the game or Fred—he was too preoccupied with the morning's events. Ever since he'd read about the escaped convict, he'd thought of little else but how to track him down. Chris closed his eyes and thought of all the things he could do with the reward money. But the money wasn't the only reason he'd become so obsessed with Hoffman. He felt a real need to prove that he could do something smart on his own. He couldn't help but feel a certain rivalry with his twin. He especially hated it when he was labeled "the jock" and Ryan "the scholar." He suspected that if Ryan put his heart into it, he could be just as good, if not better, at sports than himself. Whether he could make the same grades as Ryan was a different story.

He just *had* to find Hoffman. Even if Billy and Ryan helped him track Hoffman down, Chris knew he'd still get most of the credit. Heck, they'd probably become heroes overnight! Maybe the mayor of Lakeview would thank them personally. And his dad would be so proud of him . . .

Suddenly, an image of his brother sitting in his dad's study came to mind instead. *I can't believe you, Ryan*, Chris thought impatiently, *I thought we were going to do this ourselves!*

His brother was going to tell their dad about the convict! Chris pulled off his headphones in alarm and searched the street for Fred, whistling frantically. When the Lab came running, Chris took off for the house. If Ryan told their father about the knife and the stolen backpack he

would ruin everything! Their father might laugh
and say it was nonsense, but then again, he could
forbid them to return to the Maguire's barn.
Probably his dad would notify the police himself,
and then Chris knew he'd never get the hero's
reception he'd been dreaming about. He had to
stop Ryan before he said too much!

Flinging open the backdoor to the kitchen,
Chris raced inside the house, forgetting completely about Fred. Rounding the corner, he
sprinted down the stairs to the basement.

"What was it you wanted to talk to me about,
son?"

"I . . . I wanted to tell you . . ." Ryan's heart
was pounding. Why couldn't he get the words
out? "I wanted to tell you that . . . I'm going to
enter the *Tribune*'s photography contest."

What? Why did I say that? Ryan asked himself.
Confused, Ryan looked up to find his brother
staring at him from across the room. Chris gave
him the thumbs up sign, and Ryan blinked his
eyes. What had just happened? He hadn't meant
to say those words at all!

"Yeah, isn't that great, Dad?" Chris said,
approaching the desk. "Ryan got some great
nature shots at Billy's farm this weekend that
I've been encouraging him to enter."

Mr. Taylor frowned, looking from one boy to
the other. "Why, yes, I'm glad you're going to
enter, Ryan. But I get the feeling you wanted to
talk to me about something else." Mr. Taylor
turned to his computer. "Now boys, do you think
you can give me a few hours to write before your
mother comes home?"

"Dad?" Ryan said quickly, before Chris could interfere. "Just one more thing."

"Yes, son?"

"Do you know anything about that guy Hoffman who broke out of prison on Friday?"

Mr. Taylor looked pleasantly surprised. "I didn't realize you boys actually read anything in the paper besides the sports pages." Running his hand through his salt-and-pepper hair, he smiled reassuringly. "Yes, I know about Hoffman. But I don't want you to worry, son. Joe Hoffman is not going to come anywhere near this neighborhood. The police will find him and put him away where he can't hurt anyone." Their father glanced at his computer and sighed wistfully.

Ryan felt Chris's eyes boring into him. "Okay, I was just wondering," he mumbled.

"Come on upstairs, Ryan," Chris said. "I need your help on a current events assignment."

Ryan turned to go. "See you later, Dad," he added uncertainly.

"See you later," echoed his father. "And stay out of trouble."

I think it's already too late, Ryan thought to himself as he followed Chris up the stairs.

"How did you get me to do that?" Ryan asked as Chris shut the door of their bedroom. "That was really weird."

"What do you mean? I didn't do anything. Great minds think alike."

"You stopped me from telling Dad about the evidence we found!" Ryan cried.

"You were going to tell him we thought it was Hoffman, weren't you?" Chris confronted his brother.

"You bet—I thought it was the right thing to do."

"Listen, trust me for once," Chris pleaded. "Give me—give us a chance to see if we can dig up any more evidence that he's hiding out at Maguire's farm before you say anything to anyone." Ryan was silent. "Please?" Chris persisted. "This is really important to me."

Ryan sighed. "Okay, you win," he said, sinking down onto his bed. He fell back against his pillow and stared up at the ceiling. How had he let Chris get the upper hand in this mess? Ryan knew he should try to convince his twin that he'd bitten off more than he could chew, but he knew it wouldn't do any good. Besides, he's rather go back to assembling his portfolio of photographs.

"That's Mom's car coming up the driveway," Chris said suddenly. "I forgot all about Fred! He must be wandering around the house somewhere!"

Ryan sat up quickly. "And I never had the chance to ask Dad about him!"

"Mom says to come down to the kitchen immediately!" Lucy shouted to them from the stairway. "She's found Fred and she's really mad."

The twins made it to the kitchen in record time. Lucy had already been sent down to the basement to get her father, and their mother was standing at the sink with her arms crossed. Ryan looked around and saw with horror that the kitchen looked like a disaster area. A large bag of dog food was spilled across the floor, there were dirty pawprints everywhere, and his mother's best apron was in shreds, with some of the material still in Fred's mouth.

"Did you boys want to talk to me about something?" their mother asked, pointing to the muddy pawprints on the front of her silk blouse.

SIX

"You know, it went pretty well considering . . ." Chris said under his breath as he got up to clear the dinner table.

Ryan grinned. It was true, convincing their parents to keep Fred had been much easier than he'd thought it would be—as soon as he and Chris offered to put up allowance money to get their mother's blouse dry cleaned. However it was Lucy who was mostly responsible for their getting to keep the Lab. She'd argued that she needed a dog to protect her when she was alone in the afternoons.

"I still don't think it's fair that I have to wash dishes if I set the table," Lucy protested, licking the ice cream plates as she carried the family's dishes over to the sink where Ryan was standing.

"Oh, yeah? Say that again," Chris teased, twirling a wet dish towel menacingly in her direction.

Lucy squealed with delight. "You better not hit me or I'll tell!"

"No you won't pumpkin head!" Chris taunted.

"Mom and Dad are in the den and it's going to stay that way." He snapped the dish towel dangerously close to her, and Lucy scooped up some ice cubes from the freezer tray and hurled them at her brother.

"Stop that, Lucy," ordered Mrs. Taylor, who had appeared in the doorway. "Chris, I think there's a call for you."

"You think?" Chris asked, puzzled, the dish towel hanging lifelessly at his side.

"Well, it sounds like Billy and he asked for 'the big jock,'" his mother replied, raising an eyebrow.

"Then you know it couldn't be for Ryan," Chris chuckled, ducking out of the room as his twin pretended to gag.

"Where's Fred?" Lucy asked.

"Your father's outside in the front yard with him," her mother replied. She smiled at her daughter. "You're very fond of Fred, aren't you?"

Lucy nodded. "You like him, too. Admit it, Mom."

"Of course I do, darling. He's going to be a lot of work, but I'm glad the boys brought him home today. He's going to be wonderful company for you—and for the whole family. And," Mrs. Taylor added with a smile, "I think the responsibility of owning a pet will be good for all of you."

"Ryan, come up here!" Chris yelled. "I need help on my math homework."

Plodding up the stairs, Ryan wondered what Billy had told Chris that was important enough to warrant being disguised as a math problem.

"That call was from Maguire," Chris confided

excitedly, shutting the bedroom door. "Guess what? He saw some tracks near the old tool shed, where he keeps that motorcycle he's fixing up. The tracks—a man's footprints—were fresh, and Billy said they were too large to belong to his father."

"Are you sure they weren't yours, big foot?" Ryan joked referring to his brother's size nine feet.

"I wasn't anywhere near there today, and you know it," Chris said. "Now listen up. I told Billy about the *Tribune* article and he's really excited. We decided to meet tomorrow at lunch. You and I are supposed to check out the newspaper in the morning. Maybe there will be some more news about Hoffman—"

"But Dad told us everything he knew at dinner tonight," Ryan interrupted him.

"I know but something might happen tonight," Chris said. "Whatever you do, don't ask Dad any more questions, or he'll get suspicious."

Ryan rolled his eyes. "First I'm not enthusiastic enough, then when I try to help you by pumping Dad for information, you get mad at me." Ignoring his twin, Chris opened his closet door and began searching through the mess on the floor. "What are you looking for?" Ryan asked.

"My binoculars," Chris muttered.

"They were *our* binoculars, and you supposedly lost them last summer," Ryan reminded him. Suddenly there was a mournful howl from the garage.

"Boys!" came their mother's voice from down the hall.

"I'll take the first shift. You can check on him later," Chris said, as he headed down the hall.

"Great. I'm bushed," said Ryan. Turning out the light, Ryan yawned loudly and crawled into the cavelike warmth of his blankets. It had been a long day, and he just couldn't keep his eyes open, not even to study for tomorrow's math test. But math and everything else seemed less and less important as he drifted off to sleep.

He had to hurry, Ryan realized. There wasn't much time left. He had to find it soon. He stopped walking and stood there for a moment. He couldn't remember what he was looking for—he only knew it was important that he get there soon. Ryan squinted in the semidarkness, trying to find a landmark. All he could see were trees, looming up before him like dark, unfriendly giants. He was lost!

An eerie howling broke out in the distance, and he shuddered as his heart began to beat more quickly. *Stay calm*, Ryan told himself. The feeling that something was approaching him from behind grew stronger, and he spun around to check. Nothing was there. A gray fog was settling in, and Ryan glanced down and saw that his feet were covered with the swirling mist. A feeling of panic swept over him. If he couldn't see anything below his knees, he couldn't tell what was crawling around on the ground beneath the mist. He heard the howling again, only this time it was closer. And he was all alone.

Where was Chris? Ryan started to run, but the

fog was rising thick and fast, obscuring his vision.
The howling was growing closer. He tried to pick
up speed, willing himself to run faster, but his
legs felt heavy as lead. They grew so heavy he
could hardly lift them, as if they were stuck in
cement. Horrified, Ryan realized he was going to
be sucked down into the mist—and into the jaws
of the howling werewolf.

Suddenly a path appeared before him, leading
to a house! His legs magically free, Ryan ran
toward the house. But when he got there, he
couldn't find the door. There was no way in! The
stench of the werewolf's hot breath choked him
as the huge beast rose up behind him. In a few
seconds those sharp, cruel claws were going to
slice into his flesh.

Turning without warning, he was inside. A
long dark hallway stretched out before him. A
voice broke the silence. Softly at first, but
quickly growing louder, the voice cried out, "Be
careful! Be careful!" As Ryan listened, a door
opened at the other end of the hallway, revealing
a small room flooded with light. He heard
familiar voices inside and walked toward them.
To his right a staircase appeared.

He heard a faint barking, and wondered if it
was Fred. A movement from down the hall
caught his eye. A figure stood in the doorway. It
was Chris! Overjoyed to see his brother, Ryan
started forward. But Chris held up his hands as if
to stop him, his face a mask of fear. Pointing to
something behind Ryan, Chris cried, "Look out!"

Ryan whirled around just in time to see the
flash of the knife as it plunged toward him.

* * *

"Nooooooo!" Ryan sat up in his bed, panting with fear.

"Are you okay?" Chris asked from the other side of their bedroom.

Ryan took a deep breath, trying to still his racing heart, and wiped his forehead with the cuff of his pajama sleeve. "Yeah. It was just this scary dream I had—I thought I was a goner."

"Me, too. But I didn't know how to warn you—I couldn't talk or anything. I was waiting for you forever, and when you got there I was so relieved. Then, before I even saw the knife . . ."

Ryan turned toward his twin. "Wait a minute. Were we having *the same dream*?"

Chris's breath came out in a rush. "I . . . I guess we were."

Suddenly spooked by the darkness, Ryan reached over to his bedside table and turned on the light with a shaky hand. He stared at his twin, and Chris stared back. A moment later, Ryan climbed out of bed and went into the bathroom to get a drink of water. Afterward, he sat down at the foot of Chris's bed. "This isn't the only time we've had the same dream," he began.

"Really? I can't remember—it must have been a long time ago," said Chris.

"Well, it's never been this intense," Ryan pointed out.

Chris searched his memory. "Yeah, I usually don't have nightmares like that." He sat propped up against his pillow with his legs bent, his arms resting against his knees. A lock of blond hair fell into his eyes, and he blew it back impatiently. "That was weird, though. What does a dream like that mean?"

"I don't know. Everyone has nightmares, I guess," Ryan replied, absently rubbing the edge of Chris's blanket between his fingers. He blinked, looking around the room. Already the memory of his dream was fading, and he was glad.

"It's hot in here," Chris observed, "and Mom told me once that you can get bad dreams if you're too hot. Let's open a window."

"Hey, why didn't you do anything to save me?" Ryan burst out. "If you knew I was going to get it, why didn't you warn me, you creep! I could have been killed!"

Chris' mouth dropped open. "I did warn you. I said, 'Look out!' didn't I?"

"But not until it was too late!"

"It's not like I can control myself in my dreams," Chris argued. "Why didn't you get there faster? Geez, what ingratitude. I shouldn't have said anything at all. I should have sat there and let you get stabbed in the back!"

With one quick motion, Ryan grabbed his pillow and hurled it at his brother.

Chris lunged out of the way and snatched his own pillow, ready to retaliate. Swinging it around like a baseball bat, Chris grinned triumphantly as the pillow found its mark, throwing Ryan off balance. Growling delightedly, Ryan grabbed his cushioned headrest from the floor and threw it across the room.

Chris ducked. "Haa! You missed again, klutz!" he cackled. Forgetting the late hour, he scrambled across his bed and tackled his brother. "Truce," Chris panted, "truce, okay?"

Crouched on the ground before him, Ryan

nodded, trying to catch his breath. He looked up
at his twin again.

"Want to raid the refrigerator?" Chris asked.

SEVEN

Chris scanned the room for Billy and Ryan. As usual, Marshall Junior High's cafeteria was a zoo during the lunch hour. Holding his tray steady, he maneuvered his way through the aisles and toward the area where his brother and Billy sat, the morning newspaper tucked under his right arm. Ducking as a spitball shot by, passing a bench of soda can-crunching seventh graders, and waving at a rowdy table filled with his soccer teammates, he crossed the war zone, doing his best to keep his Sloppy Joe intact.

"Lose track of time?" Billy asked as Chris set down his tray. "I thought I said twelve-fifteen."

"Sometimes I have more important things to do than take orders from you," Chris replied calmly. He handed over the paper. "Here's the latest on Hoffman." He took a swig of his chocolate milk, then dug into his plate of french fries. "Nothing new here, but Dad did tell us a few interesting things last night."

"Hoffman's really a sleazy guy," Ryan began. "He was born in Kansas City, dropped out of high

60

school, got picked up for shoplifting at fourteen, and has been robbing and stealing ever since."

"Most of his Kansas City contacts aren't here any longer," Chris said. "Some have died—like this Mafia guy whose wife they talked to—some have gone to jail, and others just can't be found."

"Contacts?" asked Billy.

"People he knew or did business with," Chris explained.

"Who cares about them?" Billy asked.

"We care because Joe Hoffman wasn't the only one who robbed that bank five years ago," Chris said. "Two guys were involved in the heist. Only Hoffman was caught, the other guy got away with all the money, which was never recovered. They thought they knew who Hoffman's partner was—a guy named Dex Summers—but they never proved it. Meanwhile, even though he's not under arrest, Summers has disappeared."

"But they think Hoffman knows where Dex is. After all, if Hoffman can find Dex, he can get his share of the money," Ryan added.

"But here's the best part," Chris confided. "I told you about running into Jack at the grocery store?"

Billy nodded.

"Jack told us that someone had been shoplifting at the store, and he thought it was this weird guy who had come in on Saturday. His boss was blaming Jack for the missing goods, and Jack was all bummed out. Ryan and I thought that the thief might have been Hoffman—after all, that grocery store is the closest one to your farm—and we called Jack this morning and told him to check the photo in the Sunday paper."

"And?" Billy said, breathlessly.

"Jack said the guy *was* Hoffman!" Chris hissed.

Billy's mouth dropped open. "Then it's for real, isn't it? We're on the right track." The twins nodded solemnly. "What did he steal?"

"Oh, some food and whiskey," Chris replied. "Hoffman has to eat doesn't he? And if he broke out of prison, he wouldn't exactly have a lot of spending money for food."

"How would he have made it all the way to my farm without money?" Billy asked.

"Maguire, you have no imagination!" Chris said in an exasperated voice. "He could have easily hitchhiked or stolen someone's wallet." He leaned into the table and whispered, "Want to cut afternoon classes and head out to your place now, Maguire?"

Billy declined. "I have a geography test and then detention at three."

"So cut them," Chris urged.

"*Cut detention?* Are you crazy? Then I'd get a zillion more!" Billy protested. "Get your brother to go with you."

"Mr. Honor Roll?" Chris scoffed.

"I'll go with you after school at three-thirty," Ryan said much to Chris's surprise.

His twin beamed. Then his face fell. "But I have soccer practice then."

"You'd miss classes but not soccer practice?" Ryan asked in disbelief.

Chris's voice was defensive. "Hey, I have my priorities, but I'll compromise this one time," he added, as if he were doing Ryan a favor.

* * *

"I still think it's crazy to do this on our own," Ryan burst out, "but I don't want you getting into trouble without me—"

"Oh, great, you're just coming along as a babysitter then?" Chris said angrily.

"That's not what I meant," Ryan explained. "I've been dreaming about what I'd buy with the money just like you have—I've even got a lens picked out down at Hall's camera store. It's just that I don't know if it's worth it . . ." he paused. "What if something happened to us, Chris? This isn't a game—Hoffman's a dangerous man. Do you ever think about how Mom and Dad would feel if . . ." his voice trailed off, as he looked up at his brother expectantly.

"Listen, why don't we all go out together after soccer practice," Billy suggested, looking a little pale. "My dad can pick us up."

"Nothing's going to happen to us," Chris said confidently, looking from one boy's face to the other. "We won't do anything unless all of us agree on it, okay?"

"Sounds good to me," Billy said, glancing at Ryan.

Ryan was silent. "Count me in," he said finally.

Chris slapped his twin on the back and smiled. "What's our plan for this afternoon then?"

"Why don't we take a quick look around the property?" Ryan suggested.

"We can't walk around my whole farm, that would take hours," Billy told him.

"We'll just look around the house and the barn

and any other good hiding places where Hoffman might be," Ryan replied.

"Your tool shed would be a great hideout, Maguire!" Chris broke in. "You could—"

Suddenly Billy cleared his throat. "Don't look now but some g-i-r-l-s are coming over here," he warned.

The twins looked up, but it was too late to move, too late to do anything but sit there and smile as Dede Davis and Wendy Fleming approached the table. With her short dark hair and wide impish grin, Dede looked as if a speeding locomotive couldn't stop her from sitting down at the boys' lunch table. The twins knew from experience that Dede was not someone they could easily ignore—she was a cheerleader on and off the playing field. Because she had taken to biking by the twins' house several times a week during the summer, they had sort of gotten used to her. Chris especially didn't mind her company, as long as Ryan was around too. But today was another story. He didn't want her hanging around listening to their plans.

When he saw that her friend Wendy Fleming stood behind her, Chris almost groaned out loud. Wendy was the smartest girl in the class, and probably the prettiest too, but she was impossible to talk to. She wasn't stuck up, but she turned bright pink whenever she talked to a boy— especially if the boy was Ryan. Rolling his eyes, Chris, glanced at his brother, who looked as bored as Chris was uncomfortable.

"So how's it going?" Dede chirped, setting her tray down on their table. "You don't mind if Wendy and I join you, do you?"

"Sure . . ." Ryan began. But when he saw the expression on her face, he realized his mistake. "I mean, no, we don't mind, it's okay with us. Right, guys?"

"Hey, Wendy," Billy said, his voice suddenly lower by several octaves. "Why don't you come sit next to me?"

Chris wished he could sink into the floor. Their meeting was ruined. He wondered why he was surprised—this was what happened when girls showed up. Ryan lost his cool and Billy started acting stupid. Now what was he supposed to do?

"Thanks, Billy," Dede said as she sat down and pushed Wendy down beside Ryan on the bench. She turned to the twins. "Did you two have a fun weekend?"

Chris smiled. That was an easy question. Maybe he could relax now. "We camped out on Billy's farm, and Ryan told a great werewolf story."

Wendy's face lit up. "Mr. Altman read us a great story in English that Ryan wrote." Her cheeks filled with color, contrasting sharply with her white lace collar. "I thought it was really good," she finished, her voice almost a whisper.

"Well, thanks," Ryan said, slightly embarrassed.

"I bet camping out was fun," Dede sighed. "The most exciting thing that happened in our house this weekend was our hamster, Hamlet, got out of his cage and ran away."

"Did you find him?" Chris asked, totally bored.

"Yeah, we had to lure him out into the open by setting a trap," Dede explained. "We kept hearing him in the bedroom closet, but we couldn't see him. So I brought out some lettuce and carrots and a few pieces of popcorn, and pretty soon he came out."

"That's it!" Ryan burst out.

"That's what?" asked Dede, looking a little startled.

Ryan grinned widely—Dede had just spelled it out for him. If Joe Hoffman was still on the Maguire farm, they could lure him out of hiding with some sort of bait. Ryan could already think of a dozen things Hoffman would need desperately like money and food. Looking at his watch deliberately, he stood up.

"I mean, that's it for me," he said quickly. "I'm taking a test next period, and I want to go over my notes."

"But Ryan, you have study hall with me next period," Wendy pointed out shyly.

"Oh," Ryan could feel himself growing flustered. "I guess I got confused. That's right, my test isn't until later this afternoon."

"Then stay until the end of lunch," Dede told him. "You can go over your notes next period. Besides, I wanted to ask you to a pre–football game party Wendy and I are having at my house this Friday. My brother Brad plays on the high school team, you know—"

"They're on a winning streak, aren't they?" Chris broke in.

"Haven't lost a game yet," Dede boasted. "Anyhow, come around six for chili. We'll hang out, listen to music, maybe play some pool and Ping-Pong. Then we can go over to the high school together to watch the game."

"Sounds great," said Chris, for the three of them.

"Terrific!" Dede beamed. "We'll look forward to seeing all three of you then."

"I'll bring my motorcycle and give rides," Billy said.

The girls exchanged worried looks, and Ryan burst out laughing—maybe the party wouldn't be so bad after all.

EIGHT

"So what else did Mom say when you called her after practice?" Ryan prodded his twin as they pulled their bikes from the back of Mr. Maguire's pickup truck.

"Well, she said Dad told her the *Tribune* got a lead on where Dex Summers is," Chris said. "Also, that creep Jack Moses was quoted in the paper. He took all the credit for identifying Hoffman, even though *we* put Hoffman's picture in front of his face."

"Chris, who cares about Jack? Where is Dex?" Ryan asked.

"They think he's in California," Chris said.

"If Dex is in California, why would Hoffman be here?" Ryan wondered aloud as Billy led them into the orchard shop for cider and doughnuts.

Chris shrugged. "Maybe Joe doesn't have enough money to get to California. Maybe he's got a friend in Kansas City who's going to help him out. I don't know. All Dad told Mom was that they finally got ahold of Dex's old landlady in Kansas City who gave them his forwarding address, a post office box in Los Angeles."

"Not much to go on," Ryan commented.

"They're checking it out," Chris told him, grabbing a handful of doughnuts to eat as they headed up the hill toward the barn. Billy found a Frisbee, and tossed it to Chris.

"Watch out for the mud!" Ryan called as Chris jumped up to catch it.

"Hey!" Chris said, snapping his fingers. "I've got an idea. We never did decide whose wallet we were going to use to lure Hoffman out of hiding. I say that whoever drops the Frisbee first has to use his as the bait." Chris ran sideways, heading toward a dry streambed with his arms up to catch a high toss from Billy. Out of the corner of his eye he saw that the streambed was no longer dry! In one swift motion, he sailed over the streambed to the other side. The Frisbee glided past him and down onto the ground a few yards ahead. Darn it! He'd lost!

Stooping down to pick up the disk, Chris' eyes widened when he saw the large, fresh footprints beside the smoldering remains of a campfire. "Hey you guys, come here!" he called out.

"Look, here's an empty whiskey bottle," Ryan observed as they combed the area for clues. Pocketing it, he added, "I bet this is from Jack's store."

"He must be here," Chris whispered, excitedly.

"But where?" Billy said. "This is like looking for a needle in a haystack!"

"It's supposed to rain again," Chris said looking up at the sky. "He's not going to want to stay out in the open overnight. I'm sure he'll head back to the barn."

"Let's check it out," Billy said, leading the way.

As they walked toward the barn, Ryan felt a growing sense of uneasiness. What if they actually did happen to surprise Hoffman when they got there? Then what were they going to do? Ryan wondered, his feelings of anxiety temporarily turning to disgust. Chris had this weird idea that they'd instantly become heroes if they could confront Hoffman face-to-face. What were they going to do? Surround him and shout, "Surrender or else!"

Inside the barn the late afternoon light cast an eerie spell. There was nothing unusual about the vast, dusky interior, but try as he might, Ryan just couldn't shake the feeling that something evil still lurked in the shadows here as he stood beside his brother and Billy. He glanced around, but nothing looked even remotely suspicious. Bales of hay lined the walls, much of it loose and scattered across the floor. Sawdust, kicked up by the boys, swirled in the air, looking like flecks of gold in the sun's setting rays filtering in through a window near the hayloft. Ryan nodded at Billy—it was time to put their plan into action.

"So Chris, do you have the ten bucks you owe me?" Billy asked.

"Yup. Just got my allowance, plus I have some extra cash from mowing lawns," Chris replied loudly. "Almost thirty bucks as a matter of fact. I've got it in my wallet, right here in my jacket pocket. But let's hang out for awhile. I'm bushed.

I'll give it to you just before we go home, all right?"

"Okay," Billy agreed.

Chris took off his jean jacket and tossed it onto a pile of hay. "It's so hot—I'm taking off my jacket," he went on, his voice still unusually loud.

"Hey," Ryan broke in. "I've got an idea. Let's go get some frogs from the pond. We'll bring them to school and scare Dede and Wendy."

"Good idea! Let's head down to the pond," Chris said enthusiastically. He glanced up at the rafters, and then headed outside with the others as planned.

"He needs the money. I know he'll go for it if he's in there," Chris whispered as they stepped outside. Ryan put a finger to his lips and motioned for everyone to find their respective hidings spots. Then he crept around to the side of the barn and plopped down onto his stomach. Scooting over to a crack in the wall, Ryan looked through it. He could just make out a few bales of hay in the dimming interior. He pulled away briefly to make sure the others were in place.

Billy had scrunched down about fifty yards away behind an oak tree. He gave Ryan the thumbs up signal, as did Chris, who lay thirty yards from Billy near the other side of the barn. Now all they had to do was wait.

If he's there, it won't be long, Ryan thought to himself. His vision was beginning to blur from staring so long through the slit in the wall. Yet nothing had moved inside. No one had come down from the loft or left through the barn door.

Chris's jacket lay in the hay, just where he'd left it.

As Ryan lay shivering in the chilly air, his legs cramped and stiff, he heard a car drive up. Then a horn honked and a stern voice called out, "Billy! Billy! Where are you?"

It was Mr. Maguire! Ryan jumped to his feet and waved his arms at Billy to go stop his father. Darn it! Mr. Maguire was ruining everything. Now Hoffman would know they'd been covering the barn from outside. Billy rose quickly and began running toward his dad. But as the pickup surfaced over the hill, Ryan and Chris realized their stakeout was over, and they went to join their friend. By the time they'd met up with Billy, however, Mr. Maguire had already spoken to his son and driven off.

Chris was angry. "What was that all about, Maguire? Do you realize your dad gave us away?"

"What did he come down here for?" Ryan wanted to know.

"To tell me he'd had a phone call," Billy mumbled. He pulled up the hood of his sweatshirt and blew on his hands. He still hadn't looked at the twins.

"And?" Chris said impatiently.

"And he wants me to come down and help close up the cider shop," Billy added, starting after the truck.

"I don't get it. What's his problem? He came all the way down here just to tell you he'd had some dumb phone call?" Chris scoffed. "And since when can't he close up the shop on his own?"

"Take a hint and leave me alone," Billy snapped. "The phone call was from a teacher—Mrs. Ziegler, in fact. That's why he was so mad. She told him she was concerned about me, Dad says. Concerned about my attitude in school."

"Oh that's nothing to worry about—" Chris began.

"Read my lips, Taylor, and take a hike!" Billy shouted. He started down the hill toward the orchard.

Chris sighed wearily. He rolled his head from side to side and rubbed his neck. "Let's go," he said softly.

"I guess there's no point in hanging around here anymore." Ryan said. "Come on, let's go home and play with Fred. Our bikes are up at the farmhouse."

"Wait. My jacket is still inside the barn. Let me get it," Chris said.

"Okay, but hurry. I'm freezing—and starving!" Ryan yelled. He watched as his twin ran up to the barn and disappeared through the door. Ryan stomped his feet and wriggled his toes to try and warm them up. After what seemed like hours, he felt furious and started for the barn. What was that moronic brother of his doing anyway? He looked at his watch, but it was so dark out now that it was hard to make out the time.

Then out of the corner of his eye he saw his brother's figure dart out of the barn door. Finally! Ryan turned around and started toward the house. But when he didn't hear Chris run up behind him, he stopped and turned back around. Chris wasn't there. What on earth was going on?

"Ryan!" came a loud whisper. Squinting into

the darkness, Ryan could just make out his brother shutting the barn door. He waited as Chris ran toward him.

"What the heck were you doing in there? First you take forever to come out, then you go back in again," Ryan stormed at his twin.

"I didn't come out and then go back in again," Chris protested. "I was in there the whole time looking for my wallet."

"Your wallet? The one in your jacket pocket?"

"I mean the one that *was* in my jacket pocket," Chris said. "The wallet is gone. I swear."

Ryan felt a chill run down his back. "Could it have fallen out?"

"I stuffed the wallet really deep in the pocket, but I searched the floor around the jacket just in case. I didn't find it." Chris looked at his brother, his large hands dangling helplessly at his side.

Ryan thought of the dark figure he'd seen squeezing through the door. "Chris, are you sure you didn't leave the barn and then go back in?" he asked.

Chris gave him a strange look. "No, of course not."

"Then let's get out of here," Ryan replied, not bothering to disguise the fear in his voice.

"But what about my money?" Chris cried. "I wasn't supposed to lose it. Not really. That wasn't part of the plan!"

Ryan grabbed Chris by the shoulders and pushed him in the direction of their bikes. "I think I saw him. I saw someone leaving the barn ahead of you! It must have been Hoffman!"

Chris's mouth dropped open in astonishment. "You're kidding!"

"No, I'm not. And I've had enough. We're going into Billy's house and call the police right now," Ryan said, his voice tight with tension.

Chris tried to calm his brother. "No, not yet. Listen, you're right big brother. It's time to go home." He pushed back the kickstand on his bike. "Come on."

Ryan didn't argue. He knew Chris wanted them to leave for all the wrong reasons, but at this point he was cold and tired and didn't care. In the deepening darkness, the twins rode swiftly toward home.

NINE

Chris, Ryan, and Billy were hanging out at Ralph's, drinking root beers and eating burgers like they did every Wednesday afternoon. Ryan felt bored as he watched his twin play the one video game that wasn't broken. Billy was eyeing one of the girls in their class when his expression suddenly changed. They had gone over the twins' experience at the barn about a million times, but they had no idea what to do next.

"Oh, no," he said, looking embarrassed, "my dad is here looking for me." He whipped around and grabbed Chris. "Come on you guys, you have to come with me or it'll look like I'm getting into trouble here or something." The three boys walked up to Mr. Maguire together. To Ryan's surprise, he wasn't angry at all.

"Sorry if I embarrassed you, Billy," Mr. Maguire said stiffly. "I was driving by and figured you would be here. It's getting dark so early now that I thought you might want a ride home."

"Thanks," Billy said, obviously surprised by his dad's thoughtfulness. "You don't mind giving

Chris and Ryan a lift too, do you?" Mr. Maguire shook his head.

"That's okay, we have our bikes," Chris said. "We'll ride home."

"All right, but be careful." Mr. Maguire noticed that his son was staring at him, and cleared his throat nervously. "I don't want you boys walking in the dark by yourselves."

Billy looked at the twins and back at his father. "Why?" he asked. "Is something wrong, Dad."

"Well, I talked to Sam's wife, Sarah Pearson, yesterday. She told me she'd seen signs of an intruder around their farm. She thought it might be one of those migrant workers—the apple pickers I hire to come work my orchard. Those people can be strange. Anyway, I called her from the shop today to see if they'd had any more trouble and Sarah told me not to worry because Sam had taken care of everything."

"What do you mean?" Billy asked.

"Sam was out of town on business, so I didn't get the exact story, but Sarah told me not to worry. Her husband had caught the guy who'd been trespassing on their property. He was a harmless bum just like we'd thought, someone who had a drinking problem and wasn't in any shape to pick apples. But when I asked her what they'd done about him—whether they'd called the police and had him arrested—she didn't seem to know. Told me her husband had taken care of it. Until I speak to Pearson myself, I don't want you wandering around the farm by yourself, Billy. If that bum is still there, he might ask you for money or bother you in some way."

Chris was stunned. He stared at Ryan, then at

Billy in disbelief. If what Mr. Maguire had told them was true, then Joe Hoffman had probably never been in the hay barn in the first place. Instead of a dangerous convict, they'd been chasing an old drunk. Even if Hoffman had camped out on the farm, which he probably hadn't, Chris knew it had to be the bum who'd stolen his backpack and wallet. They hadn't been in any real danger at all, he realized, with a sinking heart. Worst of all, he'd never get the reward money or be a hero!

With a sheepish look, Billy mumbled something about seeing them at school the next day and quickly followed his father out to the car. Chris stood there, wondering what he could say or do to convince his brother that the past week hadn't been a total waste of time.

Ryan couldn't believe it either. Chris had kept dragging him places, insisting that they had to catch the convict. Now he'd never be able to catch up with his school work. Ryan felt like a fool for going along with it all.

"This whole thing has been a wild goose chase," Ryan said, forgetting how enthusiastic he'd been about the reward money. "I've flunked a math test, been late with a photography assignment, and spent more time than I ever wanted with your obnoxious friend Billy just because tracking down Hoffman was so important to you."

"Well, I'm sorry I've kept you from doing all those important things!" Chris said sarcastically. "And I'm sorry that I wanted to share the reward money with you. Guess I'm just not as perfect as you are. What's it like to be right one hundred percent of the time? Boy, I didn't know it was such a hardship being with Billy and me. Don't worry, we'll never bother you again." Chris strode over to the bike rack, seething with anger. "And I'm especially sorry I tried to save you from becoming a study geek! Go ahead and join the nerd club! See if I care!"

Furious, Ryan jammed the key into their bike lock and jerked off the chain. Chris jumped on his bike and pushed off, the chain falling to the ground behind him with a clatter. As Ryan watched his brother go, he felt like knocking his head against a brick wall. He hadn't meant to get so mad at Chris, but after what his twin had just said, he was even angrier. Ryan was tired of Billy, tired of Chris and tired of chasing after the idea of being a hero. From now on, he was going to do his own thing. If Chris wanted to come along with him, fine.

Ryan stepped off the school bus the next morning and was just about to head inside to his homeroom classroom when he heard a girl call out his name. Turning, he saw Wendy Fleming waving at him as she climbed out of a car. As he waited for her to catch up, he watched Chris and Dede walk past him without a word. Not that Dede was being unfriendly—she was too wrapped up in Chris to notice anything. But normally his brother would have winked at him or made a funny face.

Ryan told himself that he didn't mind if his twin ignored him. In fact, it made sense that he and Chris would be spending less time together in the future; they didn't really have that much in common anymore. Without Chris's crazy schemes to distract him, he'd have more time to play his guitar, work on his photography, and even study if he felt like it. He wouldn't have to waste any more time bailing out his twin when he got into trouble, either. It all sounded great in theory. So why did he still feel depressed?

"Hi, Ryan," Wendy said, walking up to him. Ryan caught the scent of something familiar. What was it? Suddenly he knew—root beer!

"Hi," he replied, wondering if he was supposed to carry her books or something. They began walking toward the main entrance. "Did you have root beer for breakfast?"

Wendy blushed. "No, I didn't," she said, smiling shyly. "It's my lip gloss you smell. It's root beer flavored."

Ryan was fascinated. "Does it taste good?"

Wendy giggled. "Not really. You can just smell it."

"That would drive me crazy," Ryan admitted. "I'd be thinking about root beer floats all day, and I have a hard enough time as it is making it through till lunch."

"Not as hard a time as Chris does, I bet. Where is your brother this morning?" Wendy asked, looking around the school parking lot.

"I don't know," Ryan said moodily.

Wendy began to wind a finger around her ponytail. "Um, well, I just wanted to apologize to you in case Dede and I interrupted you at lunch the other day. It seemed like you were talking about something important . . ."

"Oh, don't worry about that—we're all looking forward to the party tonight."

Wendy beamed, obviously pleased. "I'm so glad you're coming." Then she paused. "Um, Ryan, I was also hoping you might be ready to turn in those pictures you took for the newspaper—the ones for the photographic essay on girls' athletics at Marshall?"

Ryan thought fast. Wendy was managing editor of the school newspaper, and he'd promised her he'd turn the photos in by midweek. Here it was Friday already, and while he'd taken the pictures, he hadn't even begun developing the prints. Well, he couldn't let Wendy down. He'd just have to stay after school that afternoon and get it done before going to the party.

"I'd planned on finishing them today," he assured her.

"Oh, good. We need them for our layout meeting this weekend," Wendy explained. "Can you bring them to the party?" Ryan nodded. "Thanks! Now it starts around six remember, and don't have dinner before you come or you won't have room for the chili."

"Okay," Ryan promised, as the bell rang. "Listen, I have to go to my locker. I'll see you in homeroom." He hurried down the corridor, dodging bodies as he ran.

Ryan reached his homeroom classroom just as everyone was settling down in their assigned seats to listen to announcements. Mrs. Ziegler, or Mrs. Zee as her students called her, was pretty decent as far as teachers went. She wasn't bad looking and it was easy to get her off the subject. Ryan liked her because she never seemed to have it out for anybody the way some teachers did. That's why he'd been surprised when Mrs. Zee had called up Mr. Maguire about Billy. Glancing over toward the M row, Ryan saw that Billy's seat was empty.

Ryan listened halfheartedly as the announcements dragged on. Suddenly the classroom door burst open, and Billy ploughed in.

"Sorry I'm late, Mrs. Zee," he said breathlessly.

"I'm sorry too, Billy," came the response. "Especially since this is the fourth time this month. Please stay after the bell rings for a moment. I'd like to talk to you."

Billy sat down without a word. But a moment later, he was twisting around in his seat, trying to get Chris's attention by silently mouthing something. Ryan, who sat just in front of his brother, couldn't make out what Billy was saying. Since no one was supposed to be talking, Billy obviously had some important news for them if he'd risk getting into even more trouble. Ryan looked back at Chris, but his twin shrugged, equally puzzled. But Billy seemed unable to wait for the bell, and a minute later he tore out a sheet of paper and started writing a note.

In a flash Mrs. Ziegler was at his side. "Billy," she said firmly, "please give me that note."

Billy stared at her, his face almost as pea green as the walls of the classroom. As quick as lightning he crumpled up the note and stuffed it in his mouth. Several girls shrieked, and some kids stood up in their seats to see better as Billy grimaced and chewed the note. Even Mrs. Ziegler didn't seem to know what to do as her pupil swallowed the forbidden note with a horrified expression on his face.

Laughter and catcalls rang out as Billy turned around and grinned at the rest of the class, while Mrs. Ziegler rapped on his desk for attention. Then she calmly asked Wendy, who was student council president, to come up to her desk and take over while she escorted Billy to the principal's office. As Wendy made her way to the front of the classroom, Ryan stared at Chris in astonishment, their feud temporarily postponed. What had Billy discovered that was so important, he wondered.

TEN

"What are they doing to him in there? He's been in there for hours," Chris whispered nervously, as he and Ryan lurked outside the principal's office, waiting for Billy to come out. They'd been standing around for ten minutes, but Billy still hadn't emerged. Chris took his third drink from the water fountain, and glanced at his twin. Suddenly the door opened and out walked Billy. Chris rushed over to his friend.

"What did you write in that note? Are you okay? What's going on?" he burst out.

"Come on," Billy said, "let's keep walking." The twins followed him, one on either side. "They grilled me for awhile, and threatened to call my dad. I've got a few more detentions—that's nothing new."

"Why did you eat the note? What did you write that was so important?" Chris wanted to know.

"That was a dumb move," Billy admitted.

"I can't believe you actually swallowed it," Ryan said, shaking his head.

"I don't mean eating it was dumb—that was kind of fun," Billy replied. "I meant writing it was dumb. But I was dying to tell you guys."

"Tell us what?" Chris persisted.

Billy stopped. "We were right about Hoffman. He was hiding out on our farm."

"*Was* hiding out?" echoed Chris. "You mean he's gone now?"

"He's gone and we blew it," Billy told them. He stood in the hallway, hitting the palm of his hand with his fist. "The guy was there the whole time, right under our noses. And he was laughing at us, 'cause he knew we wanted to get him!"

Chris felt the blood rush to his head. This was too awful to be true! "How do you know all this? Did you see him?" he asked.

"There was a note," Billy hissed. "I found it in the tool shed, where we keep all our old farm equipment." He clenched his fists, then burst out, "He stole Rita!"

"Rita?" Ryan repeated.

"His motorcycle," Chris explained. He turned back to Billy. "But you were still working on it. It wasn't running yet."

"It wasn't working until Hoffman finished fixing it up!" Billy swore, then kicked a nearby locker. "He had the guts to borrow *my* tools, get it running, and then take off in it."

"Did you bring the note?" Ryan asked.

"It's right here." Billy pulled out a crumpled piece of light blue paper and spread it out flat against the wall. It was actually a printed bus schedule, but when Ryan saw what Hoffman had scribbled across the top, his mouth fell open.

So long, punks. Thanks for the wheels and the spare change. Too bad you lost your wallet—you could have used the reward money. I guess you won't be getting it now!

"I can't believe it. He was there all the time," Chris choked.

"And we could've still gotten that reward money!" Billy said miserably. "Instead, we gave up, and he's on his way west. See, this is a California bus schedule."

"When did you find this note?" Ryan asked hurriedly.

"This morning, when I went out to the tool shed to get something for Dad," Billy replied. "I was in there yesterday, looking for a screwdriver, and the note wasn't there then. So he must have left it last night or real early this morning."

"How do you know he's actually gone?" Ryan asked. "Maybe he's still hiding out."

"Why would he tell us where he was if he were going to stick around? Come on, man, use your head," Billy snapped. "Hoffman may be mean, but he's not dumb."

"But why would he want to help us out by leaving behind this timetable," Ryan protested. "Did he ride the motorcycle to the bus station? It doesn't make sense."

"Half the fun is in the chase, I guess," Chris replied. "Hoffman likes to live dangerously." He bent over the schedule. "He's gotta be on one of these buses. Maybe we can still track him down," Chris added, but his voice lacked conviction.

"Are you kidding? How do we know which one

he took?" Ryan said, exasperated. "He could be on a dozen different buses going to California. Or he could take one going east instead, then change in some small town and head back out west again to throw us off. He could be hiding out anywhere in the country. Plus, he's got Maguire's motorcycle now, remember?"

"He's probably already met with Dex or found some way to get his money by now," Billy added.

"But Dex is in California," Chris said.

"Dex has a post office box address there and a phone number," Ryan reminded his brother. "That doesn't mean he has to be there. He could have been in . . . in Lakeview, for instance, this whole time."

"Yeah, right," Chris said, looking defeated.

"Okay, you guys got a better idea?" Ryan asked.

"Why don't we make an anonymous phone call to the cops?" Billy suggested. "We tell them what we know about Hoffman without mentioning our names. That way, none of us will get into trouble for not telling our parents this was going on."

"If we don't tell them who we are or where exactly Hoffman's been hiding out, we're not going to have anything to report," Ryan pointed out.

Billy's face fell. "You're right."

Ryan took a deep breath and turned to his brother. "Why don't we call Dad and tell him everything?"

"Why not?! Because I don't want to be grounded for the next year," Chris grumbled.

"The police have to know that Hoffman was

here," Ryan shot back. "Knowing that might help them find him before he cuts up somebody else. You wouldn't want that on your conscience, would you?"

"I was just joking, okay?" Chris said contritely. "I guess we do have to tell Dad. He'll know exactly what to do next. Beside, we've lost our chance at the reward money. So what do we have to lose? Should we call him at the office or wait until he gets home tonight?"

"Now," Ryan decided. But at that moment, the bell rang for class.

"We'll have to wait until lunch," Chris said. "We can use the phones outside the lunchroom.

"Okay. Now let's get out of here before I get another detention," Billy said nervously.

"I still say we do it now," Ryan said firmly.

Chris looked closely at Billy. "You go to class—Ryan and I will make the call."

"I guess I don't have much of a choice," Billy said, glaring at his friend as he turned to go.

"I'm glad we're talking to Dad," Ryan said. "The sooner we wash our hands of this, the better." But Chris didn't reply. Deep down inside, he still wasn't sure he agreed.

"You make the call," said Ryan when they reached the telephones, "and I'll watch for teachers and hall monitors."

"You sure like being boss these days," Chris grumbled as he dialed his father's number. "George Taylor, please.

"What? My father is *where*?" Chris cried into the receiver, straining to hear over the first-lunch period cacophony in the background. *"At the federal penitentiary in Lawrenceville?"* He listened for a moment. "So he flew there just for the day to interview some inmates? Oh, and the warden, too? Uh huh. Yeah. Wow! And he's flying back tonight?

"Hey listen, I'm his son, I told you . . ." Chris said indignantly to the person on the other end of the line. "Yeah, one of the twins—Chris. Uh, yeah, the soccer team's doing really well this year." He grinned. "Dad talks about me a lot, huh? Um, listen, I'm calling from school and I don't have much time . . . Was it important?" He hesitated and looked over at Ryan. His brother signaled for him to hang up. "No, no. Don't disturb him. I'll catch Dad tonight when he gets home. Thanks. Bye."

Chris hung up just as Billy ran up to join them.

"There was a substitute so I snuck out of class," Billy explained.

"Dad's secretary told me he's in Lawrenceville interviewing inmates!" Chris filled him in. "There are a couple of guys there who might know where Dex Summers is."

"You mean he's not in California?" Billy asked.

"It doesn't look like it. They think the post office box address was just a front," Chris explained.

"What about his phone?" Ryan asked.

"Plugged up to an answering service," Chris told them. "Anyway, Dad's coming back late tonight. We'll have to wait until then to get the scoop."

"So we go to the party tonight, have a good time at the game, and forget about all this for awhile," Billy said. "Now, more importantly, anybody know what they're serving for lunch today?"

Ryan shrugged. "I guess it's too late to go to class now. You guys might as well go to lunch. I've got an apple and a candy bar in my locker. That's better than the glop in there. I'll be in the darkroom for awhile if you guys want to find me."

Chris and Billy started for the cafeteria. "Taking the bus home at four?" Chris called over his shoulder.

"No, I'm staying late to finish up my developing," Ryan explained. "Got a batch of photos due to Wendy tonight. I'll probably walk home, or call Mom to pick me up."

"I might go to Billy's before the party," Chris told him. "Okay if we meet you at Dede's?"

Immediately Ryan felt left out, but he wasn't going to let his brother and Billy see how he felt. "I don't care. Do what you want. I'll find a ride with someone else," he said gruffly.

"Ryan . . ." Chris began hesitantly.

Billy was already halfway through the door to the lunchroom. When he looked back and saw Chris, he yelled, "Come on, there's a line!"

"See you later, Ryan!" Chris called as he hurried after his friend, leaving Ryan standing in the hallway.

Sprawled on his stomach in the den, leafing through a *Sports Illustrated*, while the latest U2 album played, Chris dug into the bag of potato chips at his side. He felt a cold wet nose nuzzle his hand and reached out to feed Fred some chips. No one had answered the ad that his father had made them place in the *Tribune*, and it looked like Fred would be with them forever. The phone rang, and he jumped up to answer it.

"Hello?" came his sister's voice on the other end of the line.

"Hi, Lucy. What's up?"

"Did you just get home?"

"No, I've been home for about an hour."

"Then why haven't you called to come to pick me up?" Lucy whined.

"Because I don't know where you are, pumpkinhead," Chris said, looking at his watch and wondering if Billy was trying to call him now.

"Didn't you read the note?" Lucy prodded.

"What note?" Chris asked.

"The one that Mom wrote."

"I didn't see it."

"She put it on the front hall table by the mail."

"I never get any mail. Why would I look there? Where is Mom, anyway?" Chris asked.

"If you'd read the note, you'd know!" Lucy told him. "Mom sold a house this afternoon, and had to see her clients. She's not going to be back until around seven or seven-thirty and Dad's out of town until late tonight."

"And where are you?" Chris asked, wondering what all this had to do with him.

"I'm across the street at my friend Sally Ward's house," Lucy told him. "But her family was supposed to leave fifteen minutes ago for a birthday party at her grandparents' house, so you've got to stay with me."

"But I was waiting for Mom to come home and take me to Billy's," Chris said, disappointed. "I was going to take Fred out there, too. He never gets any exercise."

"So go out there tomorrow," Lucy said impatiently.

"I can't. Billy's working all day Saturday and Sunday at the cider shop."

Lucy's voice began to quiver. "Well, someone's got to stay with me until Mom comes home. Sally's already late for her party. Her grandparents live on Mission Road, and her Mom and Dad want to go—"

"They live on Mission Road?" Chris interrupted. "That's right near the Maguire farm. Can they give us a ride to Billy's?"

"You mean me too?" said Lucy, hopefully.

"Yeah, of course," her brother said.

"I'm sure they could!" Lucy replied, sounding much happier. "I'll ask."

Chris smiled to himself. It wasn't hard to convince Lucy to go visit her Number One crush. He was starting to think Billy ranked up there with Bruce Springsteen. It wouldn't be a problem to take her, either. Fred would keep her occupied while he and Billy hung out. Maybe he'd find his backpack somewhere around the farm today. Or maybe he'd find something—or someone—else . . .

Lucy came back on the line, ecstatic. "They'll take us!" she said, excitedly. "But they want to go now."

"I'm ready," Chris assured her. "I'll have to take you to a party, too, for awhile. Sure you don't mind?"

For once in her life, Lucy was speechless.

"I'll leave a note for Mom," Chris continued

with a chuckle, "and she can pick you up at Dede's house—that's where the party is—when she gets back from work." He figured the girls in his class would know what to do with Lucy—they always seemed to be babysitting around the neighborhood.

He wrote a note to his mom, added a P.S. to Ryan, then dashed upstairs, Fred at his heels, to change. A moment later he heard a car honk outside, and saw the Wards' station wagon in his driveway.

"C'mon, boy!" he whistled, grabbing a handful of dog biscuits from the top of his dresser as he tore down the stairs.

As he opened the front door, he heard the phone ring. Should he answer it? he wondered. But Fred tore out ahead of him, and Mr. Ward had already gotten out of the car to open up the back door. Chris ran as fast as he could, managing to grab Fred before he ran into the street. Forget the phone—the Wards were already late for their party.

ELEVEN

"Are you sure you'll be okay?" Mrs. Ward asked, as Lucy and Chris scrambled out of the car with Fred.

"Oh, sure. Billy's expecting me. He had to work down at the cider shop, but I know he got off at five," Chris reassured her.

"I don't see many lights on in the house," Mrs. Ward said. "Do you want us to drive you down to the orchard in case they're still closing up?"

Chris heard her husband's voice from the car. "Carolyn, we're late enough as it is."

"Oh, no thanks," Chris spoke up quickly. "It's not far. Lucy and I can always walk down there ourselves. It won't be dark for awhile." Chris took his sister's hand, and they turned toward the path leading up to the farmhouse.

"Thank you, Mr. and Mrs. Ward. Bye, Sally!" Lucy called, waving to them as she scampered up the front walk. With a joyous bark Fred suddenly took off across the yard, chasing a squirrel.

Chris whistled for him. Immediately, the Lab turned around and obediently ran back to him.

"Good doggie," Lucy cooed, patting Fred and scratching him around the ears the way Chris had taught her. "I'll give you some water when we get inside," she promised as they rang the bell and waited for Billy to open the door. When no one answered, Chris tried knocking. Still nobody came. He peered through the one of the windows. It was dark inside, although the lamp in the family room was on.

"Isn't anyone home?" Lucy said, sounding worried. "I thought you said Billy knew we were coming."

Chris pulled off his baseball cap and scratched his head. "I don't understand it. He said to come any time after five, and it's almost five-thirty now. I guess I should have called first." Suddenly he remembered the ringing telephone at home. Had Billy tried calling him to cancel their plans?

"It's getting cold," Lucy whined.

"Oh, don't be such a wimp. It's only the beginning of October," Chris said wondering what he should do. He tried the front door and found to his relief that it opened easily. "Hey, it's not locked. They must be expecting us. Let's go in."

Lucy followed her brother inside. Standing in the front hallway Chris called out, "Hello! Hello, anybody home?"

"Billy? Billy?" Lucy called out hopefully. There was no answer.

"I bet they're just running late down at the shop. A lot of people probably showed up at the last minute to buy apples or something," Chris reasoned. Fred barked from the doorstep where he stood, tail wagging, a stick in his mouth. Chris laughed when he saw him. "Let's go outside and play with Fred until they come."

Wrestling the stick from the Lab's mouth, Chris drew back his arm and threw it across the lawn and over the Maguires' white picket fence. Fred shot out across the yard, and scooting under the fence, reached the stick in seconds. He trotted back to Chris, placing it proudly at his feet.

"Ohhh, lemme do that! I want him to fetch a stick for me!" Lucy cried out, delightedly. She threw the stick for Fred to fetch, and when he raced after it, she dived into a pile of leaves to hide from him.

"Go find Lucy!" Chris urged the Lab when he came back and found Lucy gone. "Go find her. She's hiding from you!" He waited, watching the dog as he began to sniff around. When a muffled giggle came from beneath the leaves, Fred made a beeline to the tree, and with a bark, began digging frantically through the pile beneath it. When the heel of Lucy's red sneaker appeared, Fred gave a victorious bark and began tugging on her laces. Lucy popped up delightedly, laughing as she pulled out the leaves from her hair.

"Lucy, it's getting late," Chris said, trying not to sound worried. "We'd better go down to the cider shop and see what's holding up Billy."

"I don't want to walk all the way down there," Lucy pouted, her chubby face flushed. "I'm tired. Can't we go in the house and wait for Billy there? And maybe get something to eat?"

Chris sighed. "Okay, you go inside. I'll run down to the shop. Find something to eat in the kitchen. There's a TV in the family room. I'll leave Fred here to keep you company, but don't let him mess up anything."

"Okay," said Lucy, starting to skip toward the house. "Come on, Fred!"

"Lock the door when you get inside!" he called out as he watched them go but his voice was lost in the wind. When Lucy shut the door from inside, he wasn't sure whether or not she'd heard him. *Oh well, it doesn't really matter*, Chris thought. *I'll be back with Billy in a couple of minutes*. Whistling, he climbed over the fence, heading down the hill from the farmhouse and toward the orchard shop.

Chris felt charged with energy. With a whoop, he began running, the wind against his back. He heard the cry of birds above him and looked up in the sky to see a cluster of wild ducks flying south. He thought about the duck blind Billy and his father had built on the farm and hoped that he'd be invited to go hunting with them sometime.

Billy was a pro at duck hunting. He and his dad got up at five in the morning and wore warm clothes and heavy boots out to the blind, where they sat drinking hot coffee and blowing wooden duck calls to lure in the birds. When one flew off from the pack and swooped down to investigate, Billy and his dad waited until the duck was low enough to aim at, then they threw back the roof of the reeds that camouflaged them and fired their shotguns. Billy claimed that nothing was more exciting than bringing down your first bird of the season.

Absorbed in his thoughts, Chris found himself at the orchard before he knew it. But when he reached the shop, he was surprised to see that it was dark inside and closed up. Walking up to a window, he peered in. Everything looked in order. He tried the door, but it was locked. Checking the parking lot, he saw no sign of the pickup. It looked as if Billy and his dad had left the farm altogether. Had Billy forgotten the plans they'd made? Well, there was nothing left to do but turn back and head for the house. He and Lucy would just have to wait for their mother to come pick them up.

It was getting dark, though. A flashlight lay on a outside windowsill, and Chris picked it up, intending to use it on his walk back. He had pulled up the hood on his sweatshirt and was taking out his gloves when he heard the faint sound of a dog barking. Could that be Fred? he wondered. Had Lucy tried to come down here in the dark?

"Fred! Fred! Here boy, I'm over here!" he called out, running in the direction of the barking. "Lucy! Lucy are you out there?"

Suddenly, the Lab appeared. As Fred ran up to him, Chris saw that he was alone. What had happened? *Where was Lucy?*

"Fred! What's the matter? How did you find me?" Chris fell to his knees and put his arms around the dog, who began licking him excitedly. When he drew away, he saw blood on his sleeve. Chris gasped, recoiling in horror. Running his hands over the dog's coat, he found no open wounds. He checked Fred's legs and paws—there weren't any cuts. That meant it was Lucy who was bleeding! She must have tried to find her way down here and fallen and hurt herself—and it was all his fault!

How could I have left her alone like that? Chris wondered, flooded with guilt. Remembering the hide-and-seek game they'd played earlier, he cried out to Fred, "Find Lucy, boy! Take me to Lucy!"

Barking in an agitated sort of way, Fred shot out from under him and began running back toward the house. Chris followed, numb with fear. He never thought he'd be so worried about his bratty little sister. If only he'd stayed at home with Lucy until his mom arrived. If only this wasn't really happening to him . . .

As he ran toward the house, stumbling over rocks and twigs, Chris suddenly thought of his twin. *Ryan, where are you? I need your help!*

Without warning Fred swerved to the left and ran over to a small building that Chris recognized as the Maguires' tool shed, where Billy had been fixing up his motorcycle. Chris hurried over, half limping from a cramp in his leg that he'd got from running too fast. Fred began sniffing around, pawing at the ground and whining.

"Lucy?" Chris called softly. "Lucy?" he said again, a little louder. The shed only had three walls and a roof. He crept around to the open side and cautiously shone his flashlight into the dark interior. It was hard to see anything, so much junk littered the floor. His light illuminated old tractor tires, rusty scraps of metal, a few broken chairs, and . . . Chris took a step forward, his heart racing. Had something moved beside the workbench? Fred growled, and Chris felt a prickling sensation shoot up his spine. He shone his light down toward the ground . . .

His backpack!

Suddenly the pack moved, and something scuttled out from underneath it. Chris cried out involuntarily as the thing darted past him. It was a rat! Grimacing in disgust, he made his way over to his pack and saw what had attracted the rodent. Cupcake wrappers and an empty potato chip bag lay in the sawdust beside it. Hoffman must have brought his backpack in here, where he'd hidden out for a time while working on Billy's bike. But none of that mattered now because Lucy wasn't in here, and Hoffman had left the farm . . . Or had he?

Oh, no, Chris thought, his heart pounding with fear. He remembered Mr. Maguire's story about the bum. But had it really been a bum? "Oh, no!" he cried out loud this time. Had they been wrong again?

TWELVE

Ryan cleaned up the darkroom, pleased with the work he'd done. He was ready to quit and head over to the party. After emptying the tray of developing fluid, he felt a sharp cramp in his leg, much like the kind he got when he went running and hadn't warmed up properly. He bent over and rubbed his calf. Maybe he'd just been standing up in here too long. Then another cramp like a charley horse hit him, and an image of Chris popped into Ryan's mind.

Chris? Where was he now? What time was it? Ryan glanced at his watch and saw to his surprise that it was already quarter to seven. He been so absorbed in his work that he'd completely lost track of time. His brother and Billy would already be at the party by now. But as Ryan hurried to finish up, another sense of urgency about his twin washed over him. He had to get out of there quickly. *Something must be wrong*, he thought, I'd better call home.

Locking the darkroom door behind him, Ryan jogged down the deserted school corridor. He reached the pay phone outside the lunchroom and, with a shaking hand, reached into his pocket for some coins. Darn it! All he had were a few crumpled up dollar bills.

With a mounting sense of panic, Ryan ran outside and got on his bike. Pedaling faster than he ever had before, he was wheezing when he finally got home. He saw with relief that his dad's car was in the driveway. Pushing the door open, he called out for his father. When no one replied, Ryan's heart sank. His dad wasn't home. Someone else must have driven him to the airport. But where was his mom? And where was Lucy? Moving into the front hallway, his glance fell upon two pieces of white paper—notes from his mother and Chris!

He read them quickly. His mother's note said she was at work and should be home by seven-thirty. Chris's note said he'd taken Lucy with him to Billy's, and that Mr. Maguire was going to drop all three of them off at the party. Ryan was to meet them there. Ryan checked his watch. Since it was seven now, they should be at Dede's. But he'd call Billy's house first just in case they were still there. When he got no answer at the Maguire farm, Ryan pulled out the school directory, looked up Dede's number, and dialed.

"Hello," came a woman's voice.

"Is Chris Taylor there?" Ryan asked.

"Just a moment, please." He heard muffled voices and laughter in the background.

"No, he isn't here," said the woman, a minute later.

Ryan's heart began to pound. "Um, this is his brother, Ryan. Did he call or anything, or show up and then leave? Is Billy Maguire there?"

"I don't know if Billy is here either, dear. You'll have to wait a moment." Ryan waited for what seemed like forever, then he heard Wendy's voice on the other end of the line and breathed a sigh of relief.

"Ryan?" she said.

"Listen, Wendy, I'm sorry I'm late, but I've got to find my brother and Billy. Haven't they shown up at all?"

"No, they haven't."

"And they haven't called?" Ryan asked.

"Only much earlier," Wendy replied. "Chris called around five o'clock to ask if he could bring Lucy for awhile. But they never showed up. We're eating dinner now, and we're going to be leaving soon for the game. I guess you guys aren't going to make it?" She asked, her voice filled with disappointment.

"I don't know, Wendy," Ryan said. "Listen, I don't want to scare you, but I think something's happened to Chris. And Lucy's probably with him. They're in trouble, and I've got to find them."

"In trouble? What's wrong?" Wendy gasped. "Are you alone? Do you want me to get my mom?"

"No, don't get her! It might be nothing at all," Ryan said. "It's just a feeling I have, I might be wrong, but I have to follow up on it." He closed his eyes, trying to figure out what he was going to do. He thought he heard Chris calling out his name, and he jumped into action. "I think something's happened at the Maguire farm," he told Wendy. "I'm going out there now."

"How will we know if everything's okay?" Wendy asked breathlessly. "I think I should tell somebody!"

"Don't tell anyone yet! I don't want to start a panic if nothing is wrong!" Ryan ordered. He didn't understand or know how to explain these feelings he got, and he was afraid Wendy's mom would think he was crazy if he tried to tell her. "Wendy, I'll call you from the farm. Don't say anything until my mom comes to pick up Lucy. If you haven't heard from me by then, tell her what I've told you. Have her drive out to the Maguire farm. Tell her . . . tell her Chris and I know that Joe Hoffman has been hiding out there."

"You mean the guy who escaped from prison?" He could hardly hear Wendy, her voice was so faint.

"Yeah, we almost caught him, but he got away. At least that's what we thought. Maybe . . . maybe we were wrong—listen, I'm running out of time. Remember what I told you to do."

Ryan slammed down the receiver. He knew he might be grounded for the next two years or he might even get arrested for what he was about to do, but he just didn't have a choice. He grabbed his dad's car keys from the kitchen drawer where they were kept and ran out to the driveway. Settling himself in the driver's seat, he discovered that his feet could barely touch the pedals. Darn it! How was he supposed to slide this thing up closer?

With a jerk, Ryan brought the seat up so quickly that his chest hit the steering wheel. With a trembling hand, he fitted the key into the lock. It stuck halfway. He pushed it harder. *Come*

on. Come on, he thought. *Get in there. Turn!* But
it wouldn't work, and he didn't want to jam it. It
must be the wrong key, he realized, pulling it out
to examine it. Where was the right one?

Chris followed Fred back to the farmhouse. As
the Lab scooted under the fence that bordered
the yard, Chris stopped himself before scrambling after him. He wanted to see if any cars were
parked outside the house. None stood in the
driveway or anywhere else he could see. It didn't
look as if anyone had arrived. Wrenching his gaze
back toward the farmhouse, Chris noticed that a
few lights had been turned on inside. Then a
movement just inside the dining room window
caught his eye. That must be Lucy! he thought
excitedly. *She must be okay.*
    Hurrying to the front door, Chris found it still
unlocked and flung it open, calling out his sister's
name. He ran down the carpeted hallway toward
the dining room.
    "Lucy!" he shouted, rounding the corner.
    But suddenly he felt a pain like a soccer ball
had been kicked in his face at too close range and
then everything went black.

Turning the key chain over in his hand, Ryan
found another silver key that resembled the first.
He tried it and found that this one fit perfectly in
the lock. With a trembling hand, he turned the
key in the ignition and started the car.
    Stay calm, he told himself, nervously. But he
hadn't driven since the summer, when Billy had
spent several hours one Saturday teaching them
to drive on the dirt roads around his farm. Ryan

figured it couldn't be too much harder to drive down the city street.

But after heading the wrong way down a one-way street, going through a red light, and almost hitting another car, Ryan knew he'd seriously misjudged his driving ability. It was much harder to drive in traffic! But once he got on the highway leading out to the farm and figured out how to turn his headlights down from bright to normal, he started to feel more confident. Several police cars passed him, their sirens howling and red lights flashing, and he wondered if there was an accident somewhere.

Then, without warning, Ryan felt as though someone had taken a sledgehammer to his head. Reeling from what felt like a blow, he pulled the car over to the side of the road. Stunned, he sat there for a moment, frightened and confused. He knew he hadn't been hit so what had just happened? *Chris is hurt*, he realized suddenly.

Ryan started the car again, jamming his foot down on the gas and speeding blindly toward the farm, the smell of burnt rubber in his wake.

As Ryan drove wildly toward Billy's house, a sick feeling came over him. What would he do once he got there? Was he wrong telling Wendy not to spill the beans?

At first he missed the turnoff to Maguire's farm. Ryan was so used to sitting in the back seat while someone else did the driving, that he'd never really paid attention when their mother drove them to Billy's. It was dark out now, making the short drive seem like a long journey. When Ryan realized his mistake, he made a U-turn on the highway and quickly found the entrance. He pulled over just inside the fence and tried to think. Although he couldn't see it, Billy's house was several hundred yards ahead, completely obscured by the trees bordering the winding dirt road. He wondered if he should drive up to the house. In case there was any trouble he figured he should lie low, so he parked the car on the grass instead.

Ryan climbed out of the car, feeling strangely calm. His head no longer ached, and the feeling of panic was gone. He felt curiously distanced from the situation, as though his mind were floating up above him, watching his body walk toward Billy's house. The few night sounds he heard seemed to be muffled, almost as if he had cotton in his ears. Why was it so silent? Ryan wondered.

Suddenly he stumbled, turning his foot as he fell. It hurt, but he picked himself up again and began walking. He stumbled once more and looked down only to find that he couldn't see his feet through the fog. He had to get off the road, or else he'd keep on tripping over potholes. He stepped onto the grass. Under the trees, the earth was soft and carpeted with leaves, and Ryan walked swiftly and soundlessly through the mist. Soon he reached the clearing where the farmhouse stood.

A gunshot suddenly broke the silence, jolting him to attention. Someone had fired a gun from inside! Ryan began to run toward the house, his heart pounding with fear. If only he wasn't too late. Something ran into him, practically knocking him over. He realized with sudden clarity why he felt as if he were watching, instead of participating in what was happening. This was the dream he and Chris had shared—the search, the fog, this feeling of urgency! But as he waited for the werewolf's jaws to sink into his leg, he heard instead the jingle of dog tags and felt a cold nose brush against his hand. Ryan wrapped his arms around the panting dog.

"Fred! Fred! I'm so glad to see you," he cried. "I don't know how you got away, but you've got to help me now, boy. Chris is inside that house, and I bet Lucy is too. We've got to get them out!"

THIRTEEN

Chris sensed that someone was bending over him. He felt a warm breath on his cheek. Somewhere around him he heard an explosion, and he struggled to open his eyes, but his head ached terribly. Fighting the urge to slip back into unconsciousness, Chris forced himself awake. The sharp light from a nearby lamp irritated him, and wincing at the pain in his head, he closed his eyes again and started to roll over.

But something stopped him. He couldn't move his hands—they were tied behind his back, bound by rough, prickly rope as were his feet. Anger surged through him as he threw himself over onto his stomach and pushed himself up onto his knees with his chin. He blinked his eyes, and when his vision cleared, he saw that he was in the Maguires' family room. His sister, also tied up, was curled up in a ball a few feet away from him.

"Lucy," Chris whispered. But when he felt something cold and hard pressed against his forehead, he stopped short. The gun forced him to raise his eyes and meet the gaze of a man that, despite cuts and bruises and a scruffy new beard, he immediately recognized. It was Joe Hoffman!

Hoffman was holding Mr. Maguire's shotgun to his head. The convict looked dirty and disheveled in his torn clothes and he smelled like whiskey. Wrapped around his upper right arm were strips of what looked like Billy's striped bedsheet. A red stain was seeping through the makeshift bandage, and Chris realized he'd been hurt.

"So kid, we meet at last," Hoffman said coldly. He had a hoarse, gravelly voice and his words were slightly slurred. "I'd rather not have had the pleasure, but thanks to your little sister who stumbled into the room while I was trying to borrow a little spending money, I didn't have a choice."

"Don't lie! You weren't borrowing the silver, you were going to steal it!" Lucy cried indignantly.

Chris winced. Of all the times to have a big-mouthed sister, this had to be the worst. Who did Lucy think she was dealing with—Mr. Rogers? They'd be lucky to get out of here alive!

"Shut up, brat!" Hoffman yelled, and Lucy shrank back in terror. "You talk too much. The first shot was a warning, the next one's gonna go right through you, unless you do what I say."

Chris gritted his teeth against the fury that erupted inside him. This guy was threatening to shoot his sister! He instantly regretted all the times he'd wanted to kill her himself. But Hoffman wouldn't really do that, would he? A new feeling of fear swept over Chris as he realized that the man in the room with them was not only crazy, but much more dangerous than he had believed him to be.

"Lucy," he said quietly, "you'd better do what Hoffman says."

Lucy's eyes grew wide. She stared at their captor. "You mean he's the guy everyone's been looking for—the one who escaped from Lawrenceville prison?"

Hoffman stared back at her. "So even an ankle-biter like you heard of me?" He reached out with one of his large, dirty hands to pinch her cheek. Lucy cringed and instinctively Chris strained against the rope that bound him. He had to protect Lucy, but how? He needed a weapon. If only Billy and his dad would come home. Where in the world were they?

"Where are the Maguires?" Chris asked, frightened for his friend.

"How do I know?" Hoffman snarled. "They drove away over an hour ago."

Relief washed over Chris. At least Billy was safe!

"Where do you get off, punk, asking me questions?" he growled. "You're lucky I didn't bash your head in completely. I'm surprised you're awake and talking. You must have a thick skull, kid, because that wasn't a love tap I gave you."

Chris could feel a tender bump throbbing at the top of his forehead. In spite of himself, he smiled.

Hoffman looked down at him with an expression of disgust. "You and your friends thought you were such hot stuff tracking me down—what a joke! You never even got close. I knew you were out there all the time. I could have knifed you all in your sleep that night in the barn. Don't know why I didn't. I'd have saved myself a lot of trouble."

"So that *was* your knife we found?" Chris asked.

"It was one of them," Hoffman countered. Unexpectedly he winced and supported his injured arm with his good hand. Pulling a bottle of whiskey down from the bookshelf, Hoffman took one slug, then another. The blood stain on his arm had almost soaked through the cloth, and Chris realized that Hoffman must be bleeding heavily. He hoped that losing a lot of blood would weaken the convict. And while the whiskey might numb the pain, it would also get him drunk and disoriented. *I might still have a chance*, Chris thought.

But where was Fred? he wondered, remembering his dog with a pang. He looked at Lucy and silently mouthed, "What happened to Fred?". Lucy shrugged and nodded toward the window. If the dog had run away, maybe he'd be smart enough to go for help! But when Chris stopped to consider how far away they were from civilization, his cramped shoulders sagged. And how would Fred make some stranger understand him anyway? As he stared disconsolately out the window, a face appeared on the other side. Chris's heart nearly leapt out of his body.

It was Ryan!

Chris jerked his attention back to Hoffman to make sure the convict hadn't seen his brother. But the convict's back was to the window, and he seemed unaware of anything but his whiskey bottle. Chris closed his eyes and felt a wave of excitement. Ryan was here! Now all his twin had to do was sneak into the house and call the police. They were going to be saved!

He glanced at Hoffman, who was mumbling to himself, and then leaned toward Lucy. "Has anyone tried to call?" he whispered.

Lucy swallowed, her eyes large in her small, pale face. "He cut the lines," she answered in a shaky voice.

Waves of disappointment washed over Chris. He searched the window again for his brother, but the face on the other side was gone.

Chris listened carefully, and thought he heard the faint sound of a door opening and closing. *I'm going to lose my mind*, Chris groaned inwardly. There was no way to tell if Ryan had actually entered the house or if his imagination was working overtime. Suddenly Chris envisioned an image of his twin creeping down the hallway to the den. He was in! Ryan had made it!

Hoffman paced back and forth across the room, drinking and mumbling to himself. What was he going to do with them? Chris wondered. If only he had Billy's baseball bat, he could use it like a club. He knew exactly where it was in the upstairs closet. He closed his eyes, imagining the precise spot. Now if only Ryan could find it . . .

The convict laughed out loud abruptly. It was an ugly sound. "Good old Dex, I never thought he had it in him."

Chris snapped to attention. "Dex Summers?"

"My old buddy," Hoffman sneered. "You know him, of course. Not by Dex Summers, but by the new name he lived under when he got married and moved to Lakeview.''

Lakeview? Chris marveled. Dex had been living right there under their noses all this time?

"I have to admit, it was clever of him," Hoffman continued. "Setting it up so people would think he'd moved to California. He fooled a lot of people—even that new wife of his who's probably come home, found him, and called the police by now.'' He chuckled. "She had no idea about his past, Dex told me. But I was too smart for him. I discovered where he was, I came here to claim my share of the loot.

"I went to prison for a robbery we pulled off together, punk. They caught me, but Dex got away. He got away with all the money. Half a million bucks. Half of that was mine, of course. My fair share. Knowing Dex was keeping it for me was the only thing that kept me alive in that stinking jail for the last five years."

Hoffman's face had grown quite pale, and he was beginning to perspire heavily even though the room was chilly. The blood from his wound had completely soaked through his makeshift bandage, and Chris and Lucy watched in revulsion as it began to drip onto the carpet.

"But he didn't have it," Hoffman continued. "Dex didn't save it for me! He thought I was going to rot in that prison for twenty-five years. He spent every penny on his horse farm. Goodbye, Dex Summers, hello, Sam Pearson!''

Sam Pearson! Chris was stunned. Maguire's neighbor was Hoffman's ex-partner! "Why did you come back here if he didn't have the money?" he asked.

"I didn't know," Hoffman said bitterly.

"But when you found out, why did you stick around here for so long?" Chris persisted. Hoffman's expression had become dazed, and it seemed safe to ask him questions.

"I cornered him. Dex said he'd been waiting for me and had my money." Hoffman took another drink. "He told me to come up to his attic where he'd stashed the money." Hoffman's face twisted into a mask of hatred and rage.

"I trusted him, and he lied to me! He led me upstairs to the third floor, then turned around at the top and pushed me down the stairs! I fell backward and hit my head so hard I couldn't see. Then he came at me with a knife. I tried to defend myself, but I wasn't quick enough and he stabbed me. He could've finished me off while I lay there bleeding on the stairs but the poor slob couldn't do it. He told me he was sorry, but he'd spent the money. The whole half million was gone. He said he couldn't kill me 'cause I was his friend. When he reached down to help me up, I grabbed his arm"—slowly Hoffman turned and looked straight into Chris's eyes—"And plunged his own knife into his heart."

Lucy screamed. With a roar of frustration Hoffman hurled his empty whiskey bottle at the wall. It shattered with a crash, and broken glass flew across the room. The convict covered his face with his hands. When he looked back up at them again, Chris knew their time was up. He would have to get to his feet quickly, and Chris began rocking back and forth on the floor until he was able to heave himself up onto his knees. He sat back on his heels, ready to spring, waiting for the right moment.

"Killing people gets easier all the time," Hoffman said menacingly. "Dex wasn't the first person I've killed, and he won't be the last," he added, picking up the gun.

"What are you going to do with us?" Lucy cried.

Hoffman stared at her. His eyes glazed, and he spoke in a voice that held no trace of feeling. "I can't take you with me. There's no room on the motorcycle." He took a step toward Lucy. "And now that I've told you what happened, I can't let you go either. Don't worry little girl," he said, pointing the gun at her. "I'm a good shot. You won't feel a thing."

There was a splintering crash, as Ryan broke through the window, smashing the glass with Billy's baseball bat. Hoffman spun around, and Chris had the few seconds he needed to jump to his feet. Aiming carefully just as he'd done in countless soccer matches before, he hurled his body head first at Hoffman's paunchy middle. He made a direct hit, and the convict fell backward with a loud groan.

But with his hands and feet still tied, Chris could do nothing to stop himself from falling head first into a table. Darkness threatened to close in on him as he lay there stunned, unable to move.

Ryan stared at his injured twin in dismay and then tried to free his pants where they clung to the broken glass. When Ryan raised his head again he saw that Hoffman was back on his feet, pointing the shotgun directly at him. He hurled the baseball bat with all his strength across the room, knocking the gun out of Hoffman's hands. It went off with a blast, the bullet whizzing over Ryan's head.

Ryan threw himself through the window into the room, rolling over broken glass onto the carpet and scrambling to his feet. The shotgun and bat lay only a few yards away, but when he sprang for them, Hoffman lunged forward, toppling him over onto his back. Pinned down by the convict's heavy body, Ryan felt a pair of huge hands close around his neck. He struggled against the agonizing pressure as Hoffman squeezed harder and harder, but it was no use. He couldn't move and he couldn't breathe . . .

Suddenly, Ryan heard Hoffman bellow with pain as the Lab attacked, pulling the convict off him. Coughing and choking, Ryan rolled over and pushed himself up, taking huge gulps of air. But he felt light-headed, and the room swam before him. He could scarcely move, much less help Fred, and he watched dizzily as Hoffman knocked the dog off him and staggered to his feet. But Fred sprang again, pushing the large man back against a bookshelf. The heavy shelf teetered, then plunged down with a crash on top of Hoffman.

He lay motionless under the shelf with only his feet and one dirty hand sticking out. Patting Fred on the head, Ryan ran to help his brother and free his sister, who was crying with relief. In the distance, he heard the howl of a police siren.

FOURTEEN

His mother couldn't stop hugging him, but Ryan didn't mind as much as usual. Never in his life had so many people made such a fuss over him. Someone handed him a mug of hot chocolate, and he turned back to his brother who stood beside him, grinning like a lottery winner.

"Are you still posing for photographers, or is that goofy smile for real?" Ryan teased. Then he whispered, "Did you find out about the reward money?"

"Who cares about reward money," Chris whispered back, continuing to smile as yet another camera flash went off in their faces. "We're heroes!"

Ryan laughed. Right now he didn't really care about reward money *or* being a hero—he was just glad to be alive. Looking around the crowded room his gaze fell upon the blood-stained carpet, and he shuddered. Hoffman, who was only knocked out by the heavy bookcase, had remained unconscious even when the police had pulled the shelf off him. Still, Ryan hadn't felt truly safe until they'd handcuffed him and taken him away. He was relieved to know that when Hoffman did wake up, it would be behind prison bars. Only this time the police chief assured him, Joe Hoffman would be there for the rest of his life.

Ryan spotted Lucy standing beside Billy and nudged his twin. They both laughed. The Maguires had arrived with the police and rushed into the den just behind the officers. Billy had seen Lucy first and had run over to untie her. Now she was calling him her "hero" and refusing to be parted from his side.

Ryan stroked Fred, who sat between them, and felt a rush of gratitude toward the brave dog, who'd saved his life.

"You're a hero too, boy," he said.

"From now on he gets steak every day," Chris said softly, scratching Fred behind the ears.

"On a silver platter," added Ryan.

Another reporter edged over to them. "Boys?" she began.

Mr. and Mrs. Taylor, who were standing near their sons, quickly intervened. "I think they need to rest just now," Mrs. Taylor said.

"They'll be happy to answer questions a little later," their father added firmly.

Ryan nodded at the reporter. He didn't want to give up his chance to be interviewed, but he felt relieved to have a break. Everything had happened so fast. The police had arrived with Billy and his father, then his parents had come, and now all these reporters. He could see more cars driving up in the yard, which was lit up like a stadium.

"It looks like the *Tribune* isn't the only paper covering this story," Chris commented happily.

Mr. Taylor shook his head and hugged both sons again.

Billy came over with Lucy following close behind. "I don't know what to say to you guys, except 'congratulations.'" Then he sighed enviously. "I can't believe I missed out on everything!" He looked at Chris. "You growing a third eye there?"

"Yeah, thanks to you!" Chris said, gingerly rubbing his forehead. "Where were you anyway?"

"Dad roped me into going to pick up more supplies for the store," Billy explained. "I called your house to tell you not to come over, but no one answered. So I left a note on the front door, but I guess the note blew away, because some reporter just found it outside in the bushes."

Lucy went over to stand by her father. "How did you get here so fast, Dad?" she asked.

"I left the prison earlier than I'd expected," Mr. Taylor explained. "The news that Dex had been stabbed was just breaking when my plane landed in Kansas City. The paper had sent a car to wait for me, so we drove directly to the Pearson farm." He looked down at his children, his face filled with emotion. "Thank heavens nothing happened to you all. I would never have forgiven myself." He reached over and picked up Lucy, holding her tightly in his arms.

"Did Hoffman really kill Dex?" Ryan asked.

"He tried," came Mr. Maguire's voice, as he walked up to the group. "But I heard that he'll be okay. When and if he does recover, I don't think he'll be doing any more horsing around," he joked, in a rare show of humor. "Most likely Dex'll be joining his old buddy in prison, for awhile at least."

"Who called the ambulance for him?" Ryan asked. "I thought Mrs. Pearson—I mean Mrs. Summers—was in town."

"She came home just after it happened and found her husband," said Billy. "The ambulance and cops came pretty quick, and that's what probably will save Dex's life." Billy looked up at his dad, and to the twins' surprise, Mr. Maguire put his arm around his son.

"I can't believe the kids were involved in this either, George," he said to Mr. Taylor. "I feel partially responsible." He gave his son an awkward pat on the back. "I'm going to try and be around a little more in the future." Billy's ears turned red at his father's words, and his freckled face flushed with happiness. "Wouldn't want these boys to keep getting into trouble."

"I still don't understand what took you so long to get here," Chris persisted.

"Dad and I would have been here an hour ago but we saw the police cars turning into the Pearsons' property on our way home," Billy told him. "So we drove in to see what was going on. When I heard about Dex and Hoffman, I thought I should tell them what I knew. While I was talking to the cops, they got the radio call about there being trouble on our farm."

"Who called the police?" Ryan asked. There was a sudden commotion at the den door, and everyone looked up. Two girls burst into the room, ignoring the officer who was trying to keep them out.

"Ryan! Chris! Are you okay?" Wendy and Dede shouted together. When Wendy saw Mrs. Taylor she waved, and to both boys' astonishment their mother hurried over, spoke to the officer, and ushered them in.

"Wendy and I told the police to come here," Mrs. Taylor explained. "Wendy told me everything you told her over the phone, Ryan, when I arrived at the party to pick up Lucy."

Ryan's mouth fell open. He'd forgotten about talking to Wendy!

"You boys must never get involved in anything like this again without telling your father and me," his mother continued. "And Ryan, don't ever ask a friend to keep that kind of information secret. Wendy was worried sick about you both!"

"I didn't know what to do, Ryan!" Wendy burst out breathlessly. "I wish I'd said something sooner, but I'd promised I wouldn't do anything until you called or your mother arrived . . ."

Ryan had to hand it to Wendy. Not many girls could even begin to keep secrets.

"Wendy didn't even tell me!" Dede piped in. "And she was so worried, she turned ghost white. Everyone at the party thought she was sick or something."

"You missed the football game and everything, didn't you?" Chris said sympathetically.

Wendy nodded. "It's okay, the other kids went. My dad didn't mind taking us out here."

Dede glanced from one twin to the other. "Boy, I never imagined you guys could get involved in anything this dangerous." A smile lit up her face. "Next time, include us, okay?"

"I don't think there will be a next time," Mr. Taylor said firmly.

The twins grinned at each other.

"All new detectives make some mistakes," Chris said proudly.

"We've learned a lot. We'll be better next time," Ryan added.

"Excuse me, sir, but the ambulance is here for the children," a young police officer interrupted them.

"I feel fine!" Chris protested.

"It's just routine procedure," his mother assured him. "Lucy and Ryan go, too."

"Will they turn on the siren for us?" asked Lucy.

"Anything you want, pumpkin," her mother replied, stroking her hair.

"You know, we've never ridden—" Chris began.

"In an ambulance before," Ryan finished.

"Last one to the stretcher gives up his share of the reward money!" Chris cried.

"You're on, Cyclops!" shouted Ryan, running to catch up with his brother who was already halfway to the ambulance.

Don't miss the next exciting
TWIN CONNECTION adventure—
in which Chris and Ryan
make a horror movie
in a haunted house!